THE
BONDED DEAD
A RINEHART SUSPENSE NOVEL

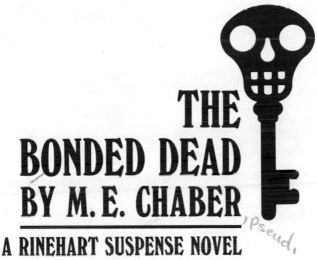

THE
BONDED DEAD
BY M. E. CHABER

'pseud,

A RINEHART SUSPENSE NOVEL

Crossen

HOLT, RINEHART AND WINSTON
NEW YORK CHICAGO SAN FRANCISCO

Published simultaneously in Canada by Holt, Rinehart
and Winston of Canada, Limited.

Library of Congress Catalog Card Number: 75-117288

First Edition

SBN: 03-085054-1
Printed in the United States of America

For Arlene and Eddie—in partial
recognition of all they have done.

M. E. C.

THE
BONDED DEAD
A RINEHART SUSPENSE NOVEL

1

The girl was no more than thirty and probably not that. Her pretty face was framed by short blond hair which looked like a halo in the light of passing cars. The man who was driving was big and handsome in a rough sort of way. Occasionally she would lift her head and laugh at something he said. If anyone had looked at them as she laughed, the guess would have been that she was in love with him. She was.

They left Miami and turned into the highway that led through the Everglades and on to Fort Myers and Punta Gorda. It was late at night and there was almost no traffic. When they reached the middle of the Everglades, he pulled over to the side of the road and shut off the motor and the lights.

"Why are we stopping here?" she asked curiously.

He reached over and put his cigarette out in the ash-tray. "I want to show you something, honey."

"What?"

"Look out the window and stare deep into the Everglades. In a minute you'll see it."

She obediently turned and stared through the window at the dark mass of the swamp.

The man checked the road in both directions. There were no visible lights. He reached over and put both hands around the girl's neck, the powerful fingers crushing down before she could even cry out. The only sound was a faint whimper deep in the strangled throat. Her body whipped around on the seat, but there was no escape from those relentless fingers.

Suddenly she slumped, her head falling forward, but he kept the grip on her throat until he was certain she was dead. Once more he checked the road in both directions, but there were no headlights. He got out of the car and walked around to the other side.

He opened the door, catching her body as it started to fall out. Lifting it, he walked straight toward the swamp. He went as far as he could without the fear of running into large numbers of snakes. He stopped in front of a pool of water and threw the body into it. He turned and went back to the car. There was still no traffic on the road.

He took her purse from the front seat. He knew that she had several hundred dollars in it. He opened it and felt around until he found the thick wad of bills. He put the money in his pocket, closed the purse and then threw it into the swamp as far as he could. He went around and slid beneath the wheel.

Starting the motor, he turned around in the road without switching on the lights until he was headed back the way he'd come. He speeded up, keeping well within the speed limit. After several miles, another car came sweeping toward him. He dutifully dimmed his lights and the two cars passed each other. He breathed a sigh of relief. It could have come along earlier.

There were only two more things to be done immediately. One would have to wait until morning, but not the other. He drove until he reached a spot where there were side roads leading off the highway. He turned into the first one, shutting off his lights as he did so. He drove slowly until he thought there was little chance of being spotted from the highway.

He reached back of the bucket seats and picked up a brown paper bag. It contained a pair of slacks, sport shirt and jacket, socks and a pair of shoes. He quickly stripped off the clothes he was wearing and put on the others. He rubbed a cloth over the shoes he'd removed so there would be no fingerprints on them and stuffed everything into the brown bag after he'd transferred what had been in the pockets.

He drove back to the highway and headed for the city. When he reached it, he drove slowly, watching until he spotted a litter basket. He pulled to the curb and tossed the brown paper bag into it.

"Mustn't be a litterbug," he said to himself with a soft laugh.

In the morning, he thought, he'd get up early and drive a few miles to a car wash place. He'd have the car washed and the inside vacuumed. That should get rid of signs of dried mud inside the car or on the tires.

That would take care of every detail—except one. The other girl.

2

I was in my office on Madison Avenue. It was late morning. There was nobody there except me. There never is. I had already poured myself a drink from the bottle of VO in the desk drawer and was sipping it while I looked over my fiscal situation. It wasn't too bad. Most of my bills were paid and I still had some money in the bank.

I'm March. Milo March. Insurance investigator. At least that's what it says on the door to my office. The only reason it's lettered there is for the benefit of the postman. I'm the only person who ever comes through that door, and if the phone rings it's either my answering service or Intercontinental Insurance Company. I keep the office so I can get mail when I'm out of town, which is often, and so I can get phone calls from the insurance company when I'm in town.

I debated for a minute which of my two callers it might be, then picked up the receiver and answered.

"Milo, my boy," he said. It was Martin Raymond, a vice-president of Intercontinental Insurance Company. They are my bread and butter, not to mention dry martinis. "How are you?"

4

"I don't know yet. I haven't had a checkup this morning."

"That's my boy," he said with a feeble chuckle. "Are you busy?"

"Not too busy to have a friendly chat with you, Martin."

"Then why not dash up here? I might have something for you."

"I'm not familiar with the word unless you mean a dash of bitters in a shot of bourbon, but I'll stroll up."

"Fine. I'll see you in a few minutes." He hung up. Martin never likes to waste time in idle chatter.

I finished my drink and left the office. I decided against strolling and took a taxi. The Intercontinental Building, also on Madison Avenue, consisted of glass and steel and looked like someone had built a psychedelic air plane and turned it into an office building after he discovered it wouldn't fly. I paid off the cab driver and went up to the executive floor.

As usual, there was a beautiful girl behind the reception desk—but a different one than the last time. This one had long black hair, large black eyes, a smooth Latin complexion and full pouting lips. The rest of her was similar to the others who had been there before as I passed through. Whoever did the hiring certainly had an eye for the finer things in life.

She looked up while I was inspecting her. When my gaze finally traveled back to her eyes, she was staring at me with a smile tugging at her lips.

"May I help you, sir?" she asked. Her voice went with

the rest of her. It made me feel as if she were running her fingers up and down my spine.

"You might," I said gravely. "I find myself at a loss in this big city. I don't know where to go—where to go for a good dinner, things like that. I thought you might take pity on me and show me around after you get off this evening."

She stared at me for a minute and then started to laugh. I waited in dignified silence for it to stop. It finally boiled down to no more than a giggle.

"I know who you are," she said. "Alice told me about you."

"Alice?"

"The girl who worked here before me. You're Milo March and you're the chief investigator here. She also warned me that if any of the other girls wanted to bet me about how soon you'd ask me for a date not to bet."

"It's nice to know I get some advance publicity. Let's change the script a little. We'll pretend that you're the stranger in town and I'll show you around."

"Several of the other girls warned me about you."

"This place is getting worse than an old ladies' sewing circle," I said sourly. "Shall we make it for dinner?"

"I'll think about it," she said. "Now, who do you want to see?"

"Martin Raymond."

She picked up her phone and dialed three numbers. She announced my name and hung up. "You may go right in."

I trudged down the long corridor that led to where Martin Raymond presided over his little domain. His secretary looked up as I reached her desk.

"Well, if it isn't the boy wonder," she said. "He's waiting for you."

I walked past her and opened the door to his private office. I stepped inside and closed the door.

"There you are," he said. He sounded as if he'd just discovered gold. That made it an important case. "Help yourself to a drink. You know where the bar is."

"I thought you'd never ask," I murmured. I walked over to an antique china closet, or something of the sort. Before it had been altered it had probably been worth a lot of money. Martin, however, had redone the inside so that it was a very complete bar. I poured myself a good-sized drink of VO and went to the chair beside Martin's desk.

"I gather," I said, "that someone has been so vulgar as to dip his fingers into the till. How much did they take you for this time?"

His face took on the expression of a worried executive. "Around one and a half million dollars."

"That's a nice place to be around. What does it involve?"

"Grand larceny."

"Well, the amount sounds pretty grand. Want to tell me the story, Uncle Martin?"

He pressed his fingers together and stared solemnly at the ceiling. "I don't have the full story, only the beginning. While we don't specialize in such policies, we do carry some insurance on brokers who handle bonds and securities. One broker to whom we have sold several policies is Drinkwater, Denkers and Murphy."

"How did Murphy get in there?" I asked.

He ignored me. "About a month ago, two young ladies

left the office at the end of their work day. The next day it was discovered that bonds and securities worth a million and a half were missing. So were the young ladies."

"I always hate to see young ladies missing," I said. "I've always thought there weren't enough of them around anyway."

"At first, it seemed simple," he continued. "Both girls were bonded, so the brokerage house had photographs of them, complete descriptions and fingerprints. Their separate apartments showed evidence of a hurried departure. They'd left behind considerable clothing, costume jewelry, more fingerprints and more photographs. The police were confident they'd have the girls within a couple of days. They had no records, so they were amateurs. As such, they would not know how to dispose of bonds and securities. Boy friends were checked out. They had gone out on casual dates with several men from the office, but they were still there and obviously just as surprised as the rest of us."

"But I gather they didn't find the girls within two days," I said.

"No, they didn't. Airlines, trains, buses, even car rentals were checked with no results, and no trace of them could be found in the city. They had just vanished. Wanted flyers, with photographs, were sent all over the country. No results."

"What about their habits outside of the office?"

"No bad habits that could be discovered. About the only social activity that could be discovered was that they occasionally went to movies. Not together. There is no evidence that they ever saw each other outside of the office. Much of the time they each went to the movies alone, but sometimes with a date who also worked in the office. Then about a week ago one of the girls showed up in Florida. Wilma Leeds."

"What did she have to say?"

"Nothing. She was dead and had been for three or four days. Her body was in the Everglades just off the Tamiami Trail. Her purse was nearby. There was no money in it except change. There was evidence that she had been living in a Miami Beach hotel under the name of Loraine Wilks. She had been choked to death. I understand that the Miami Beach police did have one or two suspects but they turned out to have unbreakable alibis."

"If the police had flyers on the girls and she had been there for about a month, how come she was never spotted?"

"Her hair was red instead of blond and she had radically changed her makeup. I understand she didn't look like the same girl. She was identified through her fingerprints."

"And the other girl?"

"No trace of her yet. She may be in Florida or she may be somewhere else—or she may also be dead. That's one of the things you have to find out."

"And the other things?" I asked softly.

"Who has the bonds and securities and arrange for us to get them back."

"I was afraid that's what you would say. How does one dispose of hot bonds and securities?"

"I believe there are only two ways. One is to sell them to someone in the Syndicate. The most you can get is fifty percent of the face value, probably less. They then may pass from member to member, each making a small profit, finally ending up in Europe. The other way is to use them as security for bank loans. As long as the loans are repaid, the bank will not report them. There is no reason to. But this means that you must have a way of investing the loan money where you will get a good and quick profit. If you can manage that, you can make a handsome profit and then still sell the bonds to the Syndicate."

"But," I asked, "aren't the descriptions of the bonds circulated to all of the banks?"

"Yes, but most houses are so far behind in their bookkeeping that it may take them a year or more to discover that the bonds are missing. It probably would have in this case except for sheer luck. Somebody in the house had a reason to check the count on one list of bonds. He went to look it up and the bonds weren't where they should have been. This started a search for the missing bonds. They were still missing when he'd finished and so were others."

"Has this list of bonds and securities been sent to the banks?"

"Yes."

"Then we can rule out the possibility that they have been put up to secure loans."

"Yes."

I groaned. "Good old Syndicate. I wish they'd stay out of my business."

For once Martin Raymond showed a crumb of humor. "Maybe they feel the same way about you."

"Yeah, but I have to look over my shoulder more than they do. What else do you have to give me?"

"That's about all I have. The police undoubtedly have more, but they haven't given us a report. The police in Miami Beach will probably have still more, but they also haven't seen fit to fill us in."

I groaned. "I should have been a public servant. On the other hand, the pay isn't very good and the tips are terrible. Which reminds me. There is a small matter of expense money."

"My secretary will give you the authorization on your way out."

I stood up. "I can take a hint, Martin. That means it's time for me to take a hike. I'll see you around." I went out and stopped by the secretary's desk.

"Hi, doll," I said. "I'm back from the upper plateau."

"I thought you might have gotten caught on one of those windy slopes," she said. "Buster, I have to say one thing for you. I don't know how you are with women but you certainly have a way with money. And that public service job the company did must have blown one of the gaskets in his head motor. Here's your loot." She handed me a voucher. I looked at it and whistled. It was for two thousand dollars. It was usually for one thousand and he'd scream about that. "I guess my natural charm is finally getting through to him."

I went down the hallway to the cashier's cage and cashed it before he could change his mind and pick up the phone. On the way back, I stopped at her desk.

"Mind if I use your outside phone for just a minute?"

"If you promise to bring it back." She pushed it over where I could reach it.

I phoned the Seven Caesars Restaurant and made a

11

reservation for two that night at eight. I replaced the receiver and pushed the phone back to her.

"Let me guess," she said. "You've been working on that new receptionist out front."

"Again it's just my natural charm. Why keep resisting it, doll?"

"The only way I'd go out with you, buster," she said, "is if I could find a suit of armor to wear. But there's a cheerful note in it. I guess I win the office pool."

"Office pool?"

"Sure. Every time we get a new receptionist we make up a pool. Will he or won't he? The won'ts have been winning recently, but I stuck with will and this time I'm the only one with that ticket."

"You have an evil mind," I said gravely.

Her inter-office phone buzzed. She reached for it.

"Tell him it's too late," I said. "I've already left with the money." I waved to her and walked down the corridor.

I stopped in front of the receptionist. "What time shall I pick you up tonight?"

She looked up and laughed. "You don't lose any time, do you?"

"That's not it at all," I said with dignity. "I'm leaving the city early tomorrow morning and I thought this could be like my farewell dinner. I made a reservation for us at the Seven Caesars for eight, but I can change the time if you'd like me to."

She leaned back in her chair—and that was quite a sight in itself. "Eight will be all right," she said.

"Where will I pick you up?"

She smiled. "I'll meet you at the restaurant."

"All right." I started to turn to the elevators, then realized something. I turned back. "You have one advantage over me."

"What's that?"

"You know my name but I don't know yours."

"It's Carmen O'Brien."

"That's quite a combination. How did O'Brien get in there?"

"My mother was Latin American and my father Irish."

"Remind me to never get in an argument with you," I said. "I'll see you at eight." I turned and went to the elevators.

Downstairs, I glanced at my watch. It was almost an hour before noon. I found a phone booth and called the police building on Centre Street. When they answered I asked for Lieutenant John Rockland. He was the head of the Special Squad.

A sergeant in his office answered the phone. I gave him my name and said I wanted to talk to the lieutenant. A moment later Johnny came on the phone.

"Hello, Milo," he said. "What do you want this time?"

"Me?" I said. "Can't I just call up an old friend?"

"You could. But you don't—unless you want something."

"I just wanted to see an old friend," I said in a wounded tone of voice. "I would like a little information if it's possible. How about lunch? Whyte's at twelve or twelve-thirty?"

"All right," he said with a sigh. "Make it twelve." He hung up.

13

It didn't give me time to do much of anything else, so I took a taxi down to the restaurant. I sat at the bar and sipped a martini until Johnny arrived. He came over to join me.

"Let's go upstairs and get a table. It'll be practically empty and it'll be easier to talk."

He nodded and we went upstairs and took a table in a corner of the front of the room. The waiter came over and we ordered two drinks.

"How's your wife and the kids?" I asked while we waited.

"Fine," he said. "Rachel was wondering the other day why you don't come out and spend an evening with us some time."

"Well, I've been pretty busy lately. You know how it is."

"Rachel said that you're a little like a mule. You have to hit a mule between the eyes with a two-by-four to get his attention, and you have to hit you between the eyes with a broad to get your attention. So if you ever do decide to come out, she's going to invite a pretty girl over for the evening."

"Well," I said, "I'm leaving for Florida in the morning. Maybe when I get back we can make a date."

He leaned back and laughed. "As usual, Rachel was right. She said that would bring you out."

The waiter brought the drinks and we were silent until he left. Johnny took a swallow of his bourbon and looked up. "You covered yourself with glory on that last case, didn't you?"

"Just luck and hard work," I said modestly.

14

"Sure. But did you ever think of something else? Here's a bunch of cops who work their heads off for a month or maybe more without getting anywhere, then you waltz in like a prima donna and solve the case right under their noses. Some day there'll be a cop so frustrated that he'll just stand up and put a bullet through your head. And it'll be called justifiable homicide. He's not only harassed by the fact that you solved the case, but he's thinking about the kind of money you make."

"Why, Johnny, I didn't know you cared."

The waiter returned and we ordered two more drinks and our lunch. "All right," Johnny said when he'd left, "what chestnuts do you want pulled out of the fire this time?"

"Remember a case about a month ago when two broads walked away with a million and a half in bonds and securities?"

He nodded. "I remember it. My squad and I worked on this end of it."

"What did you come up with?"

"You just summed it up in one sentence. We found out that the two broads walked away with the loot. Then they vanished. They didn't take a plane, a train or a bus. So they must have had a friend who drove them out of town. But we couldn't dig up a single friend who might do something like that."

"There are two other possibilities," I said. "They could have hitchhiked to some place like Philadelphia, Boston or upstate New York and then taken a plane. Or they could have taken a subway to New Jersey, bought a secondhand car from some small lot and driven away. And they probably changed their appearances before they even left New York City, so the photographs wouldn't be much good."

"We thought of all of those," he said. "How do you run a check on possible hitchhikers? Or on subway riders? You're probably right about appearance change, but do you have any idea how many beauty shops there are in Greater New York City?"

"I know. It's an impossible task. Martin Raymond told me that there are two ways of realizing money from stolen bonds and securities. Putting them up as collateral on loans or selling them to someone in the Syndicate."

"That's about it, Milo. In this case I think we can rule out the bank loan operation. News of the theft was out too soon."

"That leaves the Syndicate."

He nodded. "And it's difficult to get information there. We tried but with no luck."

Our drinks and lunch arrived and I waited until the waiter had departed. "What else?"

"It's not a new story," he said. "The minimum guess is that there is fifty million dollars worth of bonds and securities currently circulating in the underworld, and the amount is increasing each year. One of the reasons is, of course, the fact that every brokerage house is from one to six months behind on paper work. The amount of lost or stolen securities amounts to almost forty million dollars a year. It may take as much as six months to discover what is lost or stolen."

"Can't they do anything to correct this?"

"They're trying. Most brokerage houses have been buying computers to try to speed up the paper work, but it's an almost impossible task. Most of them have also installed closed circuit television to try to catch employees with sticky fingers. It helps some, but the amount is almost nothing compared to the total volume of missing securities."

"Sounds tough."

"It is, Milo. But it's not all thefts. They have something which they call fails—that is, the failure of a broker to deliver a security to a purchaser within five days. The fails will run as high as three to four billion dollars in one month. All of this is due to the paper work jam. But it also helps the thieves."

"I can see that. How many of the thieves get caught?"

"Not nearly enough," he said grimly. "Just to give you another picture of the volume of thefts, do you know why my Special Squad was working on the case you're interested in?"

"Why?"

"There is a detective squad assigned to handle security theft complaints, but they are so overworked that they can't keep up with them. My squad has been handling some and other squads have been pitching in. The solution, however, is the most difficult. You know how tough it is to pin anything on the top Cosa Nostra men. The securities that fall into their hands pass from city to city and usually end up in Europe. Even then we may hear about only a small percentage of those which are eventually peddled there."

"Well," I said, "it sounds as if I'm in for fun and games. Is that all you can tell me?"

"That's it, Milo. I can give you one more thing. We put out flyers on the two girls. If you want to come back to the office, I'll give you copies. The pictures won't mean much because they apparently did change their appearance. I don't have any photographs of the dead girl in Florida, but the stories stress the change in her looks. We haven't had any reports from the Miami Beach police. No reason to. It—or half of it—is now in their hands. I think you're in over your head on this one."

"Maybe. We'll see."

We finished lunch and I went back to Centre Street with him. Once we were in his office, he dug into his desk and handed me the two flyers. Both girls were attractive. The one identified as Wilma Leeds had black hair, although it was red when they found the corpse in Florida, I remembered. The other girl had what looked like medium brown hair. The flyers also carried their fingerprints and a list of scars or blemishes.

"Pretty complete," I said. "How did you get a record of scars?"

"The Leeds woman was a delivery cashier and the Carlton woman was a transfer clerk. When they were hired they were photographed, fingerprinted and given a medical examination. The doctor made a list of scars and blemishes."

"And you didn't uncover anything on the two women?"

"Not a thing. No criminal record of any kind. Not even a jaywalking ticket. The few boy friends they went out with were all hard-working squares. The Leeds woman was married once, but her ex-husband is in Vietnam and has been for two years. Nothing against him."

"Great," I said. "Thanks, Johnny."

"What would you like to do now?" I asked as we left the club. I knew what I wanted to do, but decided it would be too blunt to come right out with it.

"It's been fun," she said, "and I hate to put an end to it, but I do have to be at work in the morning. I think I'd better go home."

That, I thought, was more like it. I hailed a taxi and we got in. I looked at her and she gave the driver an address on Central Park West.

"Milo," she said when the cab pulled up in front of her building, "it's been a lovely evening. Would you like to come up for a nightcap?"

I thought of telling her that I never wore any sort of cap when I went to bed, but contented myself with telling her I would. I paid off the driver and followed her into the building and then to the elevator. We got off on the fourth floor. She took a key from her purse and unlocked the apartment door. We stepped into a tastefully furnished apartment. Soft lights made it even more inviting. Then, with a rude shock, I became aware that we weren't the only two people in the room. On the other side, curled up in a chair, was another girl. She was reading a book.

Carmen introduced us. The other girl was her roommate. We made idle talk while Carmen made the drinks. She gave me brandy, without asking, which was all right. Then she began telling the other girl what we'd had for dinner and what we'd seen at the club.

I sat glaring at the wall, but I couldn't think of anything to do. The roommate was a little too old for me to give her money to go out to buy candy.

Finally I submitted to fate and concentrated on the

drink, occasionally adding some profound remark to the conversation.

"Well," I said when I'd finished my drink, "I think I'd better go. I have to get up early myself to catch a plane." I stood up, and Carmen also got to her feet. The other girl looked up questioningly.

"Milo is an investigator for our company," Carmen explained. "In fact, he's *the* investigator."

"How exciting," the other girl said. "Do you carry a gun and all that sort of thing?"

"Only when I go out on a date," I couldn't resist saying. "It was nice meeting you, Kitty."

"For me, too," she said. "I'm sorry we didn't get to talk more. I'm fascinated by crime."

"To read about or to practice?" I asked gravely.

Both girls laughed and I said good night. Carmen walked with me to the door.

"Thank you for a wonderful evening, Milo," she said. "Will I hear from you when you get back?"

"I wouldn't be surprised," I said. "Good night, Carmen."

"Good night, Milo." She leaned over and kissed me on the cheek. Then I was out in the hallway.

Going down in the elevator, I laughed to myself. "Milo," I said, "you must be losing your skill."

Downstairs, I caught a taxi and went back to my apartment on Perry Street. I opened the door and stepped inside. As I closed the door I became aware that there was a piece of paper on the floor. I picked it up.

22

It had been torn out of a brown paper bag. On it, in crude lettering, there was one sentence: DEATH WILL BE WITH YOU EVERY MINUTE.

Well, at least I wouldn't be alone on the trip.

3

The plane was already winging out of Kennedy Airport before I was fully awake. The sign above the pilot's compartment went off, and I unbuckled my seat belt and lit a cigarette. I tilted the back of the seat and relaxed, waiting for the stewardess. I looked out the window, but there was nothing to see except the usual clouds. I wondered how long it would be before some genius thought of a way to put advertising on clouds. By that time they'd probably have a method of making one cloud pink, another blue and so forth. That would be a triumph for Madison Avenue.

The stewardess—a fine example of American womanhood—came tripping down the aisle. She stopped at each seat and finally reached me. "Coffee, tea or milk?" she asked.

I thought about it for a second. "No," I said. "I think I'll have a dry martini."

That got her. "Did you say a dry martini?" she asked.

"I think so. At least that's what I meant to say."

"At this hour in the morning?"

"Yes. I find it difficult to start off the day without some

fruit juice. This way I'll be able to have a healthy breakfast when we reach Miami."

Now I had her puzzled. She had obviously decided that I wasn't drunk, which bothered her more than if I had been. "And what kind of fruit juice is in a dry martini?" she asked.

"Juniper berry juice," I said, as if I were surprised that everyone didn't know that. "One of the healthiest berries in the world. It makes kings out of commoners—and sometimes commoners out of kings. It heals all the afflictions the flesh is heir to—and sometimes creates new ones. It turns every man into a hero and every woman into a raving beauty. Will you join me in one?"

She laughed and went off to return with the martini. Later, I coaxed her into giving me a second one. By that time we were old friends.

The flight to Florida is a relatively short one, and we were soon coming down at the Miami airport. I waited until the other passengers had filed past, then got up and walked to the door. The stewardess was standing there.

"I hope you had a good flight," she said with a smile.

"Thanks to you and the martinis," I said. "Otherwise I would have had to sit there staring at a bunch of stupid clouds. Maybe I can buy you that martini now?"

"I'd love to," she said, "but I can't. I have to make sure that everything is ready here for the next stewardesses and then go to the office and check out."

"A layover?"

She nodded.

"I'm going to stay at the Hapsburg House in Miami Beach. If you get thirsty, call me. Milo March."

"I already know your name, Mr. March," she said with a smile. "And maybe I will. I'm Annette Rawson."

"I'll be waiting for the call. If I'm not in, leave word where I can call you. Thanks for brightening up the trip."

I went into the terminal, picked up my luggage and got a taxi. I told him to take me to the Hapsburg House on Collins Avenue.

"Here on business?" he asked as we started off.

"Yeah."

"Hapsburg House, huh? You know, they don't allow any girls to work out of there. I'll give you my card in case you decide you want a girl while you're here."

I always get them. I decided to shut this one off. "Do you have any sexy twelve-year-olds?" I asked.

He took a startled look at me in the mirror. "What kind of guy are you?"

"Just an all-American boy," I said. "By the way, is this conversation free or do you charge extra for it?"

He got a wounded look on his face and shut up. We drove the rest of the way to Collins Avenue in beautiful silence. I went into the hotel and registered and was taken up to my room. It was a big, L-shaped room with a wide balcony overlooking the ocean. I unpacked my things and went back downstairs. It was still a little early to call the man I wanted to see, so I went into the small cocktail room just off the elevators.

It had a small circular bar. In the center of it, above the bottles, there was a mechanical hula girl whose hips worked endlessly, inspired by raw electricity. I saw the bartender was one I knew. I went over and sat on a stool.

The bartender hadn't spotted me yet, and he came over without really looking at me.

"Hello, Buck," I said.

Then he really looked at me. "Milo," he said. "When did you get in?"

"About ten minutes ago. How is everything?"

"You know. The same old thing. Everything in this town is booze, broads and bull. What'll you have?"

"A martini, I guess. It's breakfast time."

He mixed one and poured it. He looked around. "Don't tell anybody, but it's on the house. How have you been?"

"All right, I think. I never know until I find out that I've made it into the next day. And you?"

He shrugged. "The same old grind. You know how it is." His face brightened. "Say, we got a bunch of nice looking broads here right now. Mostly school teachers, I think. I'll introduce you to some if you're here around cocktail hour. I'm working a double shift today. One of the boys called in sick."

"I'll take your offer under consideration," I said gravely.

I had the martini while I cut up old touches with Buck, then went into one of the restaurants and had breakfast. After that, I phoned the Miami Beach police and asked for Lieutenant Wayne Dillman.

"Wayne," I said when he answered, "this is Milo March."

"Milo! When did you get in town?"

"About an hour ago."

"On a case?"

"Yeah. I thought you might be able to give me some information or steer me to someone who can."

"What's the case?"

"Well, it involves the girl you found in the Everglades."

"That's a dandy," he said. "I'm working on it. Come on down any time you want to. I'm only doing paper work this morning."

"I'll be right down," I said and hung up.

I took a taxi down to the police building and went up to his office. I opened the door and looked in. He was sitting at his desk, which was covered with papers. He looked up, then got to his feet with a big smile on his face.

"Milo," he said, "come in."

I went in and closed the door behind me. We shook hands.

"Good to see you again," he said. "Sit down. How have you been?"

"Fine, I guess. I've also been pretty busy."

"That should keep you out of trouble. How come you're working on this case?"

"My company carried the insurance on the bonds and securities that were stolen. A million and a half."

"That's a nice piece of change. What are you supposed to do? Get the bonds back?"

"I'm supposed to try. And to try to find out how it worked. Got anything on the case?"

"Not very much," he admitted. "When the case first broke in New York, we got flyers on the two girls from there. We checked around without finding any trace of the girls, so we more or less figured they'd gone in some other direction. Then we pulled the dead girl out of the Everglades. She'd been choked to death. The only ID on her was a Florida driver's license made out to Loraine Wilks. The address was the Coral Arms Hotel up on Collins."

"Was she carrying any money?"

"Yeah. Sixty cents. We checked the hotel and she'd been living there for about a month. When she registered she'd given a home address in Pennsylvania. We checked there and they'd never heard of her. In the meantime, the boys in the lab were checking the fingerprints. They came up with the discovery that she was really Wilma Leeds from New York City."

"Nobody spotted her from the photograph in the flyer?"

"No. I'll show you why." He opened a drawer in his desk and pulled out a photograph. He tossed it in front of me. "That's a picture of her in the morgue. Would you spot her?"

I looked at the photograph. Then I reached in my pocket and brought out the flyers. I placed the two pictures of Wilma Leeds side by side and looked at them. No one would have recognized them as being of the same woman. The hair-do was different, so were the eyebrows and the lips.

"Did you ever stop to think," I asked, "how much trouble we'll be in if men all start shaping their eyebrows and wearing makeup?"

"I've had a few nightmares about it," he said, laughing. "But now you know why we didn't make her until we got to the prints."

"What about the other girl?"

"No sign of her. Of course, she may be in another city. Or she's also changed her looks and we can't go around fingerprinting everyone."

"Any suspects on the murder of the Leeds woman?"

He sighed heavily. "Oh, we got suspects all right. Two of them, but we can't do anything about them."

"Why not?"

"They both have an ironclad alibi."

"Who are they?"

"Jack Daly," he said, "who's usually called Jack the Dipper, and Bobby Dixon, a friend of his. You've probably heard of Daly. He's had considerable publicity. He's a beach boy. He's been in and out of more police stations than you could count. Served one term of eighteen months. Dixon is just about the same story. They specialize in robbing women. Mostly jewelry, but they'll take anything that will bring a buck. Both are good-looking guys and what most people would call swingers. So there's usually an endless supply of women, especially among the older ones. We know that Daly was with the Leeds woman several times."

"So what's their alibi?"

"They both spent the night," he said drily, "playing cards with Angelo Bacci at Bacci's home."

"Bacci?" I said. "I know that name from somewhere. Isn't he a hood?"

"That's pretty accurate, but I expect Angelo would object to the term. He is now a very affluent hood. He's been arrested a lot of times on almost every charge you can think of, but he's only had two convictions. One was for possession of a gun when he was nineteen. And one conviction in Nevada. He did a year on that."

"That's where I know him from. I helped to send him up. Syndicate."

"You know it and I know it, but try to prove it. They don't carry membership cards."

"That's very interesting," I said thoughtfully. "From what I've been able to learn, the only way anyone could dispose of these securities would be to sell them to someone in the Syndicate. They must have sold them to Bacci. Then he gave them an alibi. But I don't get one thing."

"What?"

"How do you know exactly what night she was murdered? She was in the swamp several days, wasn't she?"

"She was. But we had only two rainstorms during that week. One was early one morning and the second was just about twenty-four hours later. In between the rains, someone pulled a car off the highway right where the Leeds woman was carried into the swamp and dumped her. If it hadn't been for the second rain, we could have gotten the tread marks, but they were smoothed out. No one would try to pull a murder there during the day. Too much traffic. So it had to be that second night before it started to rain."

I nodded. "Makes sense. Did you check the suspects' car or cars?"

"Yes. A blank. Daly has a new sports car, which had been washed one or two days after the murder. Dixon has a car about a year old, but it hadn't been out of the garage in a week."

"Where do they live?"

"As you cross over from Miami Beach to Miami there

31

is a string of apartment houses on the left. They live in one of those. I'll write down the address for you." He pulled over a pad and wrote on it, then shoved it over to me. I glanced at it and put it in my pocket.

"Anything else?" I asked.

"Not yet, but we're still working on it. I still think that Daly is the best bet, but I just don't have enough to pull him in."

"Sounds like all the cases, doesn't it?" I said with a smile. I stood up. "I know you're busy, so I won't take up any more of your time. Thanks, Wayne."

"Glad to help, Milo." He glanced up at me. "You will cooperate, won't you?"

"I always do, don't I?"

He laughed. "You always do, but sometimes not until the case is finished. All right, Milo, keep in touch."

"Will do." I picked up the picture and left the building. Outside, in the parking lot, I stopped to think for a minute. I did have a couple of leads, but there wasn't any evidence to throw at them. It looked as if the only way to move was to start pushing. I found the nearest phone booth and called a taxi.

When the cab arrived, I got in and gave the driver the address the lieutenant had handed me. When we arrived there, I told the driver to wait and went to the apartment. I rang the bell.

The door opened. The man who stood there wore only bathing trunks. He was tall and well muscled, his body a deep tan. It was easy to guess which one he was.

"Mr. Daly?" I asked.

"Yes. Who are you?" His voice was a flat baritone without expression.

"My name is Milo March. I work for the Intercontinental Insurance Company. Could I come in and talk to you for a minute?"

"I don't want to buy any insurance."

"I don't sell insurance," I said.

He had started to close the door, but he stopped and looked at me more closely. "What do you do?" he asked. His voice was harder than it had been before.

"I talk to people and ask questions—among other things."

He stepped back and held the door open. I walked into the living room. It was well furnished, but I could imagine that there were probably several hundred apartments furnished exactly like it.

"Sit down," he said. I took the nearest chair. He remained standing, looking down at me. "What do you want?"

"Information."

"Another lousy cop?"

"No, I'm not a cop. I'm an insurance investigator." I lit a cigarette. "I'm interested in some bonds and securities that vanished from New York City about a month ago. Two girls vanished with them. One of the girls was found here a week ago. She was dead. I think you knew Wilma Leeds, who used the name Loraine Wilks down here."

He smiled but there was no warmth in it. "So you're still a lousy cop. Yeah, I knew Loraine. I took her out two or three times. She was an easy lay. But I don't know anything about bonds and securities. And I don't know anything about her death. I already told all that to the local fuzz."

"Yeah, I know. But you still have a problem, don't you?"

"What do you mean?" he asked.

"The other girl. You have to find her, don't you, Jack? As long as she's alive, she can testify against you."

His face darkened with anger. "Take a hike. If there's anything I can't stand it's a nosy cop hanging around. And don't come back. The next time I may throw you out."

"It doesn't cost anything to try," I said. I got up and walked to the door. I stopped and looked back at him. "Maybe I should ask your friend about bonds and securities. Angelo Bacci. He ought to know."

I could tell by the expression on his face that I'd made a score. I opened the door and stepped outside, closing it gently behind me. I went down to the taxi and we drove back to the hotel.

Up in my room, I sat on the bed and thought about my visit. I'd dropped a couple of things. Once they hit the fan there should be plenty of action. That was the way I wanted it. Force them to make the moves and they were almost certain to make a few mistakes.

I checked through the papers in my wallet. My Florida gun permit was still good. I got up and removed my jacket. I got the gun and holster from my suitcase and slipped into the shoulder harness. I checked out the gun and slipped it into the holster. Then I put the jacket on. I put the two flyers and the photograph on the dresser and went downstairs. I had lunch out on the patio, then went into the bar. There were four or five people there, but I went to a spot some distance from them and ordered a brandy from Buck.

"A busy day?" I asked him when he brought it.

"About like this," he said. "Most people are out on the beach or still recovering from last night. It'll start getting busy around four. I guess you've been working."

"Yeah."

"What is it this time?" he asked.

"A little more than a million dollars and a dead broad."

He looked interested. "You mean the broad they pulled out of the swamp a week ago?"

"That's the one. Did you know her?"

He shook his head. "Only what I read in the papers after they found her. I think she stayed some place up the avenue."

"Do you know a guy named Jack Daly?"

"You mean Jack the Dipper?"

"That's the one."

There was a look of disgust on his face. "I know him. He used to be a beach boy around here. Worked at four or five hotels. He was a good-looking kid and he'd play up to the older women. He'd hold hands with them, give them a free feel, stuff like that until he got a chance to dip into their purses. That's how he got his name. Jack the Dipper. He was also a kind of half-assed pimp. I saw in the paper that he was back in town."

"He's back all right. Have you seen him?"

"He ain't been around here. I wouldn't serve him if he came. You got to do something to protect the customers. He's mixed up in your case, huh?"

"I think so. He and a friend of his named Dixon."

"I don't know him, but I seem to remember that the

two of them were arrested together on some case about a year ago."

"How about Angelo Bacci?" I asked. "Know him?"

"I don't know him. I don't get around in those rarified circles. But I know about him. He's supposed to be the number two man in the Cosa Nostra in Florida. Whatever he is, it must pay pretty well."

"Know where he lives?"

He nodded. "Everybody in Miami Beach knows where he lives. You know that kind of thin island between here and Miami? There are a lot of rich homes on it. He owns one of them. The only way to get to it is by boat. He in it, too?"

"I'm pretty sure he is."

"Better watch your step, Milo. He's got a couple of his pet gunmen with him all the time. There's been a few reported shootings over there at night, but there's never been any evidence when the cops got there."

"Does he ever go out on the town?"

"I hear he does. He's got a broad and he takes her out once in a while. Sometimes she goes out alone. Or almost alone. She's been in here a few times, but there's always been one of the gunmen playing nursemaid. I guess he doesn't trust her."

"Know her name?"

He shook his head. "The only thing I ever heard her called was Baby, but I guess that ain't her name."

"What does she look like?"

"Blond. Good looking and really stacked. I'd guess twenty-four or twenty-five. And dumb. But not too dumb to get the mink coats and the ice that goes with them. And there's something else you should know."

"What's that?"

"He's got a kind of junior partner—according to what I read and hear. A guy named Tony Antonio. I think he lives up around Hollywood. All I know is that their names are always linked together."

"Anything else you can think of?"

"Not that I remember. But they're tough boys. I hope you're prepared."

"I am." I patted my coat beneath my left arm. "When it's raining I always wear my raincoat."

"Good," he said. Then a worried look came over his face. "But I hope you've got a franchise for that thing. The hotel might take a dim view of it if you were picked up here because of it."

I laughed. "I've got the paper."

Somebody on the other side wanted a drink and Buck went off to serve him. He'd just finished when my name was called over the loudspeaker. Buck motioned to a phone that was across the room. I walked over and picked up the receiver and said hello.

She laughed. "I knew you'd be in the bar, so I told them to page you there. This is Annette Rawson. Remember me?"

"How could I forget such a groovy stewardess? I'd decided that you weren't going to call."

"I'm flying out again tomorrow," she said, "so I thought I'd call and collect that martini."

"The first thing I did," I said gravely, "was to order a martini for you. By this time the ice has melted three or four times, so I guess I'd better throw it out and order you a fresh one. And I have an improvement on the plan."

"What?"

"After the martini or martinis, why don't we have dinner together?"

She hesitated a second. "I'd like that as long as you understand that I have to be home early because I have to get up at the crack of dawn. I'm working a morning flight out of here."

"I won't like it but I'll accept it. You want me to pick you up or do you want to meet me?"

"I'll meet you."

"What time?"

"About eight?" she asked.

"I have a good idea," I said. "There is a huge balcony outside of my room which overlooks the ocean. Why don't you meet me here, we'll have appetizers and martinis on the balcony and then go to dinner wherever you'd like."

She hesitated and then said, "All right. I guess a girl ought to be safe on an open balcony."

"Either that or have broad-minded neighbors," I said.

She laughed. "All right, Milo. I'll be there at eight." She hung up.

I went back to the bar and had one more brandy. Then I told Buck I was going up to my room to take a nap and I'd see him later.

"A nap?" he said indignantly. "I thought you were working."

"I am, but a man has to get some rest once in a while. Besides, there isn't anything I can do just now."

"How come?"

"All I have are leads but no evidence. I've stirred things up a little, so now I sort of wait until some action shows up. Once it does, I'll know I'm on the right trail."

"I don't know," he said, shaking his head, "but I'd think that was a little risky considering the people you're playing around with. Suppose they just shoot you first and talk to you later?"

"In that case, don't send flowers. Just turn down an empty glass at the bar."

"An empty glass?" he asked, puzzled.

"Yes. It was said many hundreds of years ago by a philosopher and poet. He said: 'And when like Saki you shall pass, among the guests star-scattered on the grass, and in your blissful errand reach the spot, where once I sat, turn down an empty glass.' Otherwise, it's known as an after-death drink."

"Okay," he said. "I'll turn down an empty glass. Go get your nap."

"I may need it for another reason. I have a heavy date tonight."

"I'll drink to that," he said. "See you later."

I went upstairs and stretched out on the bed. I went to sleep immediately.

It was almost six-thirty when I awakened. I went into the bathroom and splashed some water on my face. Then I went downstairs. This time the bar was full and so were the tables, but I managed to find a stool at the bar. Buck came over.

"Have a good nap?" he asked.

"The best. I dreamed of great goblets of dry martinis and long-stemmed broads. Which reminds me, I'll have a martini while I wait for the long-stemmed broad."

He came back with it in a minute. "Boy, these double shifts are for the birds. But I'll still hate to see the summer end. Then the snow birds start coming in. They're too much. . . . Is she meeting you here?"

"Who?"

"The long-stemmed broad."

"Do you think I'm crazy?" I asked. "This one's a snuggle-bunny. I'm not going to bring her in here for all you dirty old men to stare at. We're to have cocktails on the balcony upstairs."

He laughed. "Look who's talking about dirty old men." He moved off to serve someone else. When he'd finished he came back. "I don't know why I didn't pick an easier job than tending bar. This is killing me."

I laughed. "I have a friend, Bo Del Monte, in California, who says that old bartenders never die, they just pour away."

"Hey, that's pretty good. I got to remember that. See the girl on the other side of the bar? The one with long black hair."

I looked. She was sitting there, nursing a drink and looking as if she were afraid someone would start talking to her. She had a pretty face and the rest of her that I could see above the bar was first class, too. "I see her. What about her?"

"She just checked in a few days ago. From somewhere up north. A little on the shy side, but I think she's lonely, too. Why don't you buy her a drink and I'll introduce you."

"You missed your real calling, Buck. You should have been a pimp. All right, I'll buy her a drink, but I told you that I had a date for tonight."

"It's better that way. You don't make a pass the minute you meet her and she'll feel safer."

The man who had been sitting next to me had left. Buck fixed a drink for her and put it in front of the empty stool. Then he went over and talked to her. I didn't look directly at her, but I could see that she was being reluctant. But Buck had a way with people and she finally got off her stool and came toward me. She looked frightened.

Buck was there by the time she reached me. "Miss Carlson," he said, "this is Mr. March. He's a frequent visitor here and a nice guy. He bought you the drink."

"Hello," I said.

"Thank you for the drink, Mr. March," she said primly.

"I thought you looked a little lost over there," I said. "But I didn't insist that you sit here to drink it. That was Buck's idea. I'm glad he thought of it. Is this your first visit to Miami Beach?"

She managed a shy smile. "It is, but I didn't know it showed that much."

"How do you like it?"

"I don't know. I haven't seen very much of it yet."

"There isn't much to see. But I like to come here once in a while."

"Are you here on a vacation, Mr. March?"

"Please call me Milo. I always feel uncomfortable when anyone calls me Mr. March. No, I'm here on business, but I manage to steal a few hours from it to enjoy myself."

"What business are you in—Milo?"

"I work for an insurance company in New York City, but we do business all over the world. Are you from up north, too?"

"Philadelphia," she said.

41

"I've been there once or twice but I don't really know the city. Would you like another drink, Miss Carlson? By the way, do you have a first name?"

"It's Betty. And I would like another drink, thank you."

I motioned to Buck and he served us two fresh drinks, a big smile on his face. Buck was always happy when he thought he'd fixed up two people he liked.

We talked some more. She told me she worked in an office in Philadelphia, that she lived alone and that she didn't have any friends except some of the people she worked with. She began to relax a little although she was still on her guard.

I glanced at my watch and saw that it was seven-thirty. "I'm sorry," I told her, "but I have to leave now. I have an appointment in thirty minutes. But I will look forward to seeing you tomorrow."

"I'll probably be here," she said. There was a smile on her face but sadness in her voice. "Thank you, Milo."

I waved to Buck and went upstairs. I called room service and told them what I wanted, including a pitcher of martinis. I sat down, lit a cigarette and waited.

The waiter was there promptly at eight, wheeling in a table covered with dishes and the pitcher of martinis. I had him put the table out on the balcony. I signed the check and he left. He was barely out of the room when the phone rang.

It was Annette. She was downstairs. I gave her the room number and she said she'd be right up. In a few minutes there was a tap on the door. I opened it and there she was. She had looked pretty great in her uniform, but a dress did much more for her.

"Welcome to my home away from home," I said. "And it's nice to meet a woman who is on time."

She laughed. "The airline teaches us that."

She was wearing a stole. I took it and draped it over the back of a chair, then escorted her out to the balcony. The moon was making a wide track across the ocean and the voices of a few swimmers floated up to us.

I held the chair for her, then poured martinis and uncovered the hot dishes. "I'm sorry," I said, "but the butler is off tonight. You'll have to put up with me."

"I never cared much for butlers anyway," she said with a smile.

I lifted my glass. "To you, Annette. The most beautiful object in the skies."

We drank, and it suddenly occurred to me that there was one false note in this romantic picture. There wasn't anything very romantic about a guy with a gun under his left arm. I excused myself and went into the room. I was going to put the gun in a dresser drawer, but realized that she might see me from the balcony. I went into the bathroom, took off the harness and hung it on the back of the door. Then I hung a towel over it and went back to the balcony.

We drank, nibbled on the tidbits and talked. She was interesting as well as beautiful. Finally I realized that the pitcher was almost empty.

"I'd better order some more martinis," I said. I stood up and leaned over her. "I'll be right back. Don't go away." Her perfume drifted up and wrapped itself around me and I was struck down. The next thing I knew I was kissing her. It was a long kiss. It lasted all the way inside and to the bed.

Later, we were lying on the bed and her head was on my shoulder. "Were we good?" she asked sleepily.

"The best," I said and meant it.

"I guess I was wrong," she said. "A girl isn't safe on a balcony."

The telephone rang. I cursed under my breath and got up to answer it. As I picked up the receiver, I was aware of her padding past me on her way to the bathroom. I hesitated and watched her walk. It was sheer poetry.

When she disappeared, I put the receiver to my ear and said hello.

"Milo March?" the voice asked.

"I think so, but I haven't looked at my ID recently. Who's this?"

"A friend. I have a suggestion for you. Why don't you take the next plane back to New York City?"

"Why?"

"I'd hate to see you get hurt."

"That's very considerate of you and I appreciate it, but I'm enjoying myself too much."

"You'll leave Miami Beach," he said and his voice was harder. "You can walk into a plane and leave or you can go in a pine box. Make it easy on yourself."

"I will, baby. Who do you work for? Bacci?"

"Smarten up, March. If you stay around we'll take you." There was a click as he hung up.

4

I got a cigarette from my shirt, lit it and sat down on the bed. I was certain that the caller had been one of Bacci's hoods. It meant that Daly hadn't lost much time reporting to Bacci and he hadn't lost much time in trying to scare me off. That meant two things. I was on the right track and Bacci would rather scare me off than try to kill me. That might give me a very slight edge, but I'd need every bit I could get.

Annette came out of the bathroom. As she passed the dresser she stopped and looked down, then picked up the photograph of the dead girl. "Who is this?" she asked.

"A girl. They pulled her out of the Everglades about a week ago. She'd been murdered. Why?"

"She was on one of our flights several weeks ago."

"She got on at Kennedy Airport?"

"She would have to. We don't make any stops on the way."

"Was there another girl with her?"

She nodded. "A blond. That's all I remember about her. They both seemed very excited, and I know I thought that it must be their first trip to Florida."

"First and last for that one. Her name was Wilma Leeds. Maybe the last trip for the other one, too."

She replaced the picture and came over to sit on the bed. "Milo," she said, "are you some kind of gangster?"

"I didn't know there was more than one kind. Why do you ask me a question like that?"

"I took a towel from the back of the door. There . . . there was a gun beneath it."

I laughed. "I'd forgotten for the moment that was where I put it. No, Annette, I'm not some kind of gangster. I am an insurance investigator and I have a permit to carry that gun."

"You're down here because of that girl?" She gestured toward the dresser.

"Yes. She and the other girl stole one and a half million dollars in bonds and securities. We believe that they had help. Not in the actual stealing but in being told what to do and in disposing of the securities. I believe that girl was killed so she couldn't be a witness. They may have also killed the other girl. If they haven't, they will when they catch up with her."

"That phone call you got just as I went into the bathroom," she said. "Was that . . . ?"

"Connected. Yes. It was somebody suggesting that I leave Florida and go back to New York."

"Are you going?"

"No. Look, honey, there's nothing to get in a flap about. I'm paid very well for my work and I'm very good at it. Also, I don't like punks—even the ones who have a lot of money."

She shuddered. "I'm cold. Let's get dressed and go out for dinner."

"I second the motion." I leaned over and kissed her on the shoulder. "Sorry, honey. I wouldn't have told you except that I decided that it was better than having you think I'm a gangster."

We were soon dressed and ready to leave. I put the pictures in the dresser drawer and called room service to tell them they could pick up what was left of the supplies. Then we left.

"Let's stop in at the bar here," I said as we stepped out of the elevator, "for one drink while we decide where you want to eat."

The bar was still busy but there were a few empty stools. We walked over and occupied two of them. I noticed as we approached the bar that Buck was sizing her up. Then he nodded his approval. He came over as soon as we were seated.

"Annette," I said, "this is Buck. He's very dependable for a barkeep. Which means if you're ever around here alone and want to have a drink, he will protect you as much as you want to be protected—and no more. Buck, this is Miss Rawson, a lady of pristine beauty and a delightful soul."

"Hello, Buck," she said with a smile.

"Miss Rawson, it is my pleasure," Buck said. "What'll you have to drink, Mr. March?"

"Knock it off, Buck," I said. "I can't stand that mister stuff. It's not my bag. Bring us two martinis. Just wave the bottle in front of the vermouth."

"Okay, Milo." He grinned as he mixed the martinis. Then he brought them over. "On the house," he said. He looked straight at me. "I'm glad to see that you're finally showing a little class, Milo." He left before I could think of an answer.

"What did he mean by that?" Annette asked.

"That was his stamp of approval on you."

"Your friend Buck seems to be a bit of a character."

"That's the understatement of the year, honey. Where do you want to eat tonight?"

"Why don't you pick a place?"

"I'm not that familiar with the spots," I said. "The only time I come down here I'm on a case and most of the time I eat here. The food is good but you deserve something special. Pick any place you want."

She glanced at me out of the corners of her eyes. "Do insurance investigators really make that much money?"

"I'm not exactly underpaid and I also have an unlimited expense account. You may consider that you are being taken to dinner by Intercontinental Insurance."

"I will think about it—providing that you guarantee that you will be the only representative present at all times."

"Especially at *all* times," I said solemnly and she giggled.

By the time we'd finished the martinis, she had made a decision. We went out and the doorman got a taxi for us. She told the driver where to take us.

It was a good choice. You could almost sense that the food was the best the minute you stepped inside, but it also had character. There's many a restaurant with good food but no character.

We had another martini each and then ordered. While we ate we resumed getting acquainted, which had been interrupted on the balcony.

We had brandy with our coffee, then Annette looked at her watch. "I'm sorry, Milo," she said, "but I'd better go. I do have to be up very early tomorrow."

"Okay, honey," I said. I paid the check and we went out and got a taxi. She gave the driver the address. "Do you have your own apartment here?" I asked as we drove off.

"Yes and no," she said, laughing. "Several of us on the New York-Miami run chipped together and rented one apartment in New York and one here. It works out fine. When I'm laying over here another girl is laying over in New York."

"Sounds chummy," I said.

We reached her building. I had the taxi wait while I walked her to the apartment. She promised to phone me when she got back. We kissed and I went back to the taxi.

When I reached the Hapsburg, I had one more drink at the bar and then went upstairs and went to sleep. The pillow still held Annette's scent and it was a nice way to go to sleep.

I was up early the next morning because there was something I wanted to do. I had a fast breakfast in my room, then put the photograph of the dead girl in my pocket. I went downstairs, got a taxi and told the driver to take me to a place where I could get copies of a photograph made. He drove down to Lincoln Road and finally stopped in front of a place. I had him wait. I went in and had several copies made. Then I had the driver take me to a store where I could buy manila envelopes. I got two and put a copy of the photograph in each one. I addressed one to Jack Daly at his apartment and the other to Angelo Bacci. I looked up Bacci's address in the phone book. Then I had the driver take me to a messenger service.

When I got back to the hotel, I went into the bar. Buck was working. I ordered a VO and water back.

"You just get up?" he asked.

"No. I've been out working. You never appreciate how hard I work."

"My heart bleeds for you. What kind of work?"

"Stirring things up. Just do me one favor. If you see a sinister-looking character walking up behind me at the bar, tip me off."

"Okay, but don't mess up my bar." He poured the drink for me and came back. "That was a swell doll you were with last night. How did you manage that?"

"Clean living," I said modestly.

"You seeing her again tonight?"

"No. She's up in the wild blue yonder by this time. She's a stewardess on a plane to New York."

"She'll be back?"

"Yeah."

"You know the one I introduced you to last evening?"

I nodded.

"She liked you," he said. "A lot of guys have tried to pick her up since she's been here, but she's a shy little mouse. But she told me she thought you were a nice guy. I didn't cop out on you."

"That's because I am a nice guy," I said modestly. "Why don't you go in business for yourself, Buck?"

He got a wounded look on his face and started polishing the bar.

"Relax, Buck," I said. "Every once in a while you get

too serious. Sure, your shy little mouse is a good-looking doll. So is Annette. I dig both of them, but I'm not down here to be the playboy of the Atlantic. I'm down here to do some work. If I get too wrapped up in any doll, someone is going to shoot me in the back. If that happens, I not only bleed easily but it smarts. Do you read me?"

"Loud and clear, Milo," he said. He grinned. "I guess I've been here so long I forget that some people do come here on business. It's especially hard to believe it in your case. You never seem to be working."

"That's the secret of hard work. Make it look easy. You've got a good eye for dolls, Buck. Why don't you go after some of them yourself?"

"My wife wouldn't like it. She's narrow-minded about some things."

The loudspeaker squawked into life and I was being paged for a phone call. I crossed the room and picked up the receiver of the house phone.

"This is Wayne Dillman," he said. "How are you doing, Milo?"

"Plugging along. You turn up anything?"

"Nothing. How come you stole that photograph from my desk when you were down here?"

"I thought you were giving it to me. You want it back?"

"No. I've got others. Why did you want it?"

"I had some copies made this morning. I sent one to Jack Daly and one to Angelo Bacci. There should be some interesting reactions to that."

"You're a damn fool, Milo. What are you trying to do? Get yourself killed?"

"I hadn't planned on it," I said drily. "It's just my way of working. I'm not like you, Wayne. I can't pick up a phone and have fifteen squad cars racing to the rescue. All I have going is a license, a gun permit and myself. And I've learned that if you can make people think they have to get rid of you, they're bound to make a few mistakes. The more they make the better for me."

"I suppose you're right," he said, "but it's a pretty risky way to work—especially when someone like Angelo Bacci is involved."

"That's why I get paid as much as I do. Don't worry. I only *seem* to be interested in nothing but booze and broads."

"I hope so," he said. "You'll keep in touch?"

"Just like you were my old worried mother. See you around." I hung up and went back to the bar.

"A broad?" Buck asked.

"No. A cop who's worried about my health."

"I'm worried about your health, too. There's reason to worry when you fool around with a guy like Angelo Bacci. He's no Boy Scout."

"I passed them up, too. Not enough money in that racket. Are you going to stand around worrying or are you going to give me another drink?"

He brought the bottle over and poured me another shot. "You're a hardheaded bastard," he said.

"I resent that," I said indignantly. "I've got the bumps to prove I'm not hardheaded."

Two other customers showed up and he went to serve them. Then someone else entered the room. I looked around. It was Betty Carlson.

"Good morning, Betty," I said. "Can I buy you a drink?"

"Good morning, Milo," she said. She sounded like she had a hangover. "I guess so. Maybe a whiskey sour." She took the stool next to me.

Buck came over and I gave him the order. He mixed the drink and brought it back. She took a sip of it and made a face.

"What's wrong?" I asked. "Too much vacation last night?"

"I think so," she said. "I was watching television and I guess I drank more than I realized."

"I've always said that television would ruin the country," I said. "Gulp that down and we'll get you some more medicine."

She swallowed it and Buck came over and refilled it quickly. She began to sip on it.

"How about having lunch with me?" I asked.

"I don't know if I can make it," she said. "Maybe after this one . . ."

She finished that drink and we went out on the patio and got a table. "I think I'd better have another drink, then maybe I can manage some soup but no more than that. I'm really not used to drinking that much."

"I sort of guessed it," I said. The waitress came over, and I ordered a whiskey sour and a dry martini. She brought them from the service bar on the patio.

"You're beginning to look a little healthier," I said.

"I feel a little better but not much. I think I'll just have soup for lunch. I'm sorry, Milo."

"Think nothing of it. Happens to all of us at some time or other."

53

I beckoned to the waitress and she came over. I ordered soup for her and a creamed chicken dish for myself. Coffee for me and tea for her.

We didn't talk much during lunch. She was occupied with getting her soup down and keeping it there, and I was watching the girls who were sunning themselves around the pool. Whenever I visit a place I like to watch the natural fauna of the region.

"Well," I said when we were finished, "do you feel any better?"

"A little but not much," she admitted.

"Think you might feel like going out to dinner with me tonight?"

"I'd love to, Milo, but I'm not sure I'll be up to it. I think I'll go up and take a nap now. Maybe that'll help. If I'm not down at cocktail hour, call my room and we'll see."

"Fair enough," I said. I paid the check and walked her to the elevator. After it had gone up, I stood there for a minute. I decided it was time to make some more preparations. I went out and found a taxi. I had him drive me to a rental place I knew from other visits.

I rented a nice, modest Cadillac sedan. If there were going to be any excitement, I didn't want to depend on taxis. I stopped off and bought some more manila envelopes and some stamps. Then I took a short drive up to the island where Angelo Bacci lived. I parked opposite it for a few minutes. It was an impressive-looking house. His name was on a mailbox beside the street and there were stairs leading down to a boat dock. A phone was in plain view on the dock. I decided that was probably a house phone so you could call him, and if you were some-

one he wanted to see, he'd send a boat for you. Neat and
gaudy.

I'd driven about two blocks, heading back for the
hotel, when I first became aware that I was being followed. The car was an Olds and there was only one person in it, but I couldn't get a good look at him. I'd have
to remember not to be careless about such things again.

I drove straight back to the hotel and turned the car
over to a boy who would park it. I went inside, made a
right turn just past the desk and walked down a flight of
stairs. There was another restaurant down there and just
beyond it a side exit covered with shrubbery. It came out
on a side street where taxis parked. I walked out far
enough to be able to see both streets, but I was still pretty
well concealed by the foliage.

He was parked across the street. He looked to be about
thirty, with a surly-looking face and blond hair. I turned
and went back to the lobby and up to my room. This
time I addressed three envelopes. The third one went to
Tony Antonio in Hollywood, Florida. I found his address
in the phone book. I put stamps on them and went down
to the lobby and mailed them. I stepped into a phone
booth and called Lieutenant Wayne Dillman.

"Milo March," I said when he answered. "Those two
gunmen that Bacci keeps around. Do you know them?"

"Like the back of my hand. But I can't do too much
about it. They have very few convictions but long sheets
of arrests. We've arrested them four or five times our-
selves, but that's as far as we got. Why?"

"Is one of them a slender guy, about thirty, with blond
hair?"

"Yeah. That's Carl Ketcher. Strictly a psycho. He's a

killer because he gets his kicks out of it. He's about as safe as a rattlesnake—maybe less so. You've met him?"

"He's following me today. At the moment he's parked just outside of my hotel. I just wondered about him."

"You want to make a charge against him?"

"For what? You know it wouldn't stick."

"You're right, of course. But watch yourself, Milo. He's dangerous."

"So is the bathtub if you don't watch where you step. The good thing about this is that I've got them stirred up. I'm going to keep stirring."

"How about me assigning a man to work with you?"

"No, thanks, Wayne. It wouldn't scare them off and it might hamper my way of working. I'll keep in touch." I hung up and went into the bar. I ordered VO and water.

I sat there, brooding. I was beginning to get somewhere. They were stirred up. The question was what would they do first. They might try to grab me and find out how much I knew before they killed me. Or they might try to lure me to some place where they could kill me without any witnesses around. The third possibility was that they might try to kill me when I was driving through an area that wasn't too congested. The last seemed the most likely. They would think they were getting me off guard, and the odds were that there would be nobody to identify them. Lieutenant Dillman might know who did it, but that would be a long way from proving it.

"What's wrong with you?" Buck asked.

"I always look this way when I'm working," I said.

"That's work?" he asked scornfully. "I've seen bums that worked harder than that."

"Each to his own, Buck. Maybe you can help me. I want to find somebody who has a boat and would take me over to the rear of Bacci's house sometime at night if I want to go. Somebody who also won't talk about our deal."

He thought for a minute, then his face brightened. "I know just the man for you. He's a nut and will probably enjoy doing it, but give him some money anyway."

"Of course."

"He has his boat docked not far from where Bacci lives. His name is Aristotle Murphy. He lives on the boat. I guess he has some small income, because he never works. He either goes out in the boat all by himself or he stays at the dock and reads. About once a month he goes out on a drunk, and that's how I met him."

"Sounds good. How do I find him?"

"You go south from that island where Bacci lives and it's the first dock on this side. His boat is named Aristotle, too."

"Okay," I said.

"Hey, I just thought of something else. You want someone who might give you some information, too, don't you? I think I have somebody. He needs the money, too. Ever hear of Speed Harris?"

"The name sounds familiar, but I don't place it."

"He used to be a jockey, one of the best. Two things put him out of business. Too much booze and too many horse bets. Speed could always ride winners, but he never could pick them. And if he only has two bucks in the world, he'll put it on the nose of some plowhorse."

"He doesn't sound like he'd have much information."

"He picks up a lot more than you'd think. He's always hanging around horse players, either at the track or at the bookie joints. Most of the mob remember him from the times they won big money on him, so they slip him a few bucks. And they talk in front of him as if he couldn't hear."

"It might be worth a try. Where do I find him?"

"He lives in a mission over in Miami. Just a minute. I got the address somewhere." He pulled out his wallet and fumbled through it until he came up with a slip of paper. "Here it is. I'll write it down for you." He got a pad and a pen from back of the bar and wrote on it. He shoved it over to me.

I glanced at it and put it in my pocket. "I'll see both of them sometime tomorrow. Make me another drink. I'll be right back." I went out to the desk and sent a telegram to Martin Raymond. I told him I was making progress and I needed more expense money. I didn't exactly need it yet, but I was sure I would, and it was better to have it in reserve than to have to wait for it.

I finished my fresh drink and went upstairs. I took off my jacket and stretched out across the bed. I was pleased with the fact that I was already getting reactions. Now all I had to do was continue pushing—and keep my eyes open. I fell asleep shortly afterward.

Two hours later I awakened. I stripped off my clothes and took a shower and shaved. I got dressed and checked my gun again before I put it in the holster. I slipped the safety off before putting it away. There might be a small amount of danger of shooting myself, but if anyone started gunning for me I didn't want to waste time.

58

I went downstairs, through the lobby and down the steps to the side exit. He was still parked across the street, smoking a cigarette and watching the hotel entrance. I returned to the main floor and entered the bar. It was the cocktail hour, but I managed to find a stool. I told Buck to bring me a martini.

"Been working again?" he asked.

"No. Taking a nap."

"Some job. All you do is sleep, hang around with broads and drink booze. And you get paid for it."

"I get time and a half when somebody shoots at me."

"I guess I wouldn't like that part of it," he said. "How's it look?"

"I guess I've made somebody nervous. There's a little man following me around. We'll see some action soon."

"Not in here, I hope," Buck said. "All those hoods are bad shots."

"But think of the publicity if it happened. There would be headlines about 'Hapsburg House shot up— bartender wounded.' It would double business for the hotel, and think of the tips you'd get for telling the story."

"Yeah," he said gloomily and moved away.

I looked around. Betty Carlson wasn't anywhere in sight. Leaving my drink on the bar, I went over and picked up the house phone. I asked for her. She answered right away, sounding half asleep.

"Milo March," I said. "How do you feel?"

"Terrible," she wailed. "I think I'd better stay in my room and be miserable all by myself. Can I have a rain check, Milo?"

"Sure, honey. Get well tonight and we'll have that dinner tomorrow night. Okay?"

"Okay," she said. "Thank you, Milo."

"Take care, baby." I hung up and went back to the bar. I had one more martini, then went out front and waited until the boy brought my car. The blond guy was still parked across the street.

I got into the Cadillac and headed downtown. The other car fell in behind me. I made several martini pit stops and finally ended up in one of the more expensive joints. I went in and had a wonderful dinner. I took my time over it and the coffee, but finally paid the check and got up.

I told the flunkey up by the door that I wanted my car brought from the parking lot. He stepped out to get one of the boys, and I saw him make a gesture with his right hand. I looked through the glass door and saw Carl Ketcher sitting in his car on the other side of the street. As I watched, he got out, hurried to a phone booth and put in a call.

He was just leaving the phone booth when my car arrived. I took my time tipping the boy and getting into the car. I didn't want the blond to get worried about losing me. Then I drove straight back to the hotel. I looked in the bar but Buck wasn't there, so I went up to my room.

I took off my jacket and hung it in the closet. I loosened my tie on the way over to the television set. I turned it on and stood there for a minute, making a big decision. Finally I decided on one nightcap before going to sleep. I called room service and asked them to send up a bottle of VO and some ice.

When I turned to go back to the bed, I saw that something new had been added. There was a gift-wrapped package on the dresser. I walked over and looked at it.

There was a card on top. On it was written: "From a friend. Good luck."

I thought about it for a minute. First, I didn't really have any friends in Miami. Second, anyone I knew would have put his or her name on it. And, third, why was it in my room instead of waiting for me down at the desk?

Foolish questions deserve foolish answers, so I didn't even try to answer them. I picked up the box and gingerly carried it out on the balcony. I looked down. There was no one on the beach. Nor was there anyone out on the adjoining balconies. I lifted the box and threw it as hard as I could. I stepped back a couple of paces and waited to see if anything would happen when it hit the ground. Nothing did, except that it rolled several feet toward the ocean.

Feeling slightly foolish, I went back into the room. Then I decided I'd wait awhile to see how I should feel. There was a knock on the door. I quickly took off my shoulder holster and stuffed it in the desk drawer. But I took the gun with me as I opened the door.

It was the waiter. I stuffed the gun into my pocket before he saw it and signed the check. I let him out. Then I got undressed, made a drink, lit a cigarette. I got into bed and turned out the light.

There was a late movie on television. A bunch of cowboys were chasing another bunch over some hills. It wasn't very exciting. If you've seen one horse run, you've seen them all. But I was too lazy to get up and change the channel. I propped a pillow behind my neck and leaned back. I sipped at the drink and smoked a cigarette and waited.

Half an hour later, cowboys were still chasing each other. I couldn't tell whether it was the same cowboys or not, but it certainly looked like the same scene. I lit another cigarette.

Then it happened.

5

There was a loud explosion and with it a brief flare of light beyond the balcony. The windows rattled. In a way it still caught me by surprise, and I glanced at the television set. They were firing guns there, but no six-gun ever made that much noise. I jumped up and ran out on the balcony.

The package was no longer where I'd last seen it. In fact, it wasn't anywhere in sight. There were wisps of smoke drifting up from the sand. I could hear voices from the other rooms and I suddenly became aware that a few people were starting to come out on the balcony. I was hardly dressed for the occasion, so I scurried back into my own room. I turned off the television set and got back into bed. There was still the solace of my unfinished drink. I lit a cigarette to go with it.

There was no doubt about one thing. The explosion had come from the package I'd thrown on the beach. The gift from a friend. I'd been suspicious of it, without being too certain of what I was suspicious about, and I'd done the first thing that came into my mind—get rid of it.

I had to admit that I was shocked. I'd had a lot of people shoot at me, and some had even hit me, but no one had ever tried to blow me up before. I suppose it was a sort of honor, but at the moment I didn't appreciate it.

Well, that was one more thing I'd have to keep in mind. It was bad enough looking for a guy who wanted to shoot me, but how did you spot somebody who wants to lay a bomb in your lap? I did have to admit one thing. I was certainly getting results from my pushing.

Finally I put out my cigarette and went to sleep. Sometime later I think I heard a knock on my door, but I ignored it and continued sleeping. It was early when I woke up. Six o'clock. I was used to that. When there started to be action on a case, I always tensed up and could never sleep many hours at a stretch.

I phoned room service and ordered breakfast, telling them to send a bucket of ice along with it. I walked over and unlocked the door, then went back to bed. I took the gun with me, holding it under the covers. It was maybe twenty minutes before there was a knock on the door.

"Come in," I called.

It was the waiter. He rolled a table in and pushed it over to the bed. "Would you like your coffee poured?" he asked.

"Not just yet, thank you."

He gave me the check and I signed it. As soon as he was out of the room, I went across and locked the door again. I went back and sat on the bed, putting the gun on the night stand. Then I made myself a drink. I needed it then. I had just realized that if I had stopped in the bar the night before, as I usually did, I would probably have entered the room just about the time the bomb went off. That was some thought to wake up with.

I ate my breakfast and had two cups of coffee and began to feel like a new man. I dressed and went downstairs. It was too early to do the things I'd planned, so I bought a paper at the newsstand and went into the bar. It was also too early for Buck. He was not yet on duty. I sat down and ordered VO on the rocks from the other bartender. I opened the newspaper and began to look through it.

There was a brief story on page three. It merely said that someone had thrown or planted a bomb in the rear of the Hapsburg Hotel. It had been a fairly powerful bomb but had gone off too far from the hotel. No damage had been done. No motive had been established and, at the moment the paper had gone to press, there were no suspects.

Buck came in and went to work. As soon as he made sure that everything was in place on the back bar, he came over. "I hear there was a little excitement around here last night."

"I just read about it. Not much to read though. The story says they have no suspects and no idea of the motive or who might be the intended victim."

"I could make a pretty good guess about the intended victim," he said darkly.

I pretended not to know what he meant. "I didn't know you had any bombers, except possibly Castro agents."

He gave me a scornful look. "Are you kidding? The Syndicate could probably come up with an atomic bomb if they wanted to. Of course, that would be a little expensive just to get one guy." He was still pushing his idea. But I was saved from doing any more acting by being paged for a phone call.

I went over and picked up the house phone. "This is Milo March," I said. "I'll take that call in here."

"Milo?" he asked a moment later. It was the lieutenant.

"Good morning, Wayne. You're up and around early this morning."

"I'm always up and around early. You know what happened?"

"You mean here? I just read about it in the morning paper."

"I'll bet. Where were you last night?"

"I went out and did a little pub-crawling, then had dinner in one of your more expensive restaurants and came home."

"What time did you get home?"

"Well, I left the restaurant about five or ten minutes before midnight, so I must have gotten here at twelve, give or take a couple of minutes."

"Did you hear the noise?"

"I was pretty tired so I went to sleep as soon as I got here. I thought I heard something once, but that was all, so I went back to sleep."

"Were you alone last night?"

"Yes. Except for the guy who's following me. What's this all about? You don't mean you suspect me of setting off bombs?"

"No, but I suspect that it was meant for you."

"Nonsense. Nobody would try that on me."

"You seem to forget," he said, "your old friends, the Cosa Nostra. They're very versatile when it comes to disposing of people they don't like. Would you like to hear my theory of what happened?"

"Of course," I said politely.

"I think that bomb was meant for you. It went off on the beach directly in a line with your room. It was undoubtedly a time bomb. Somebody knew approximately what time you would reach the hotel and set it to go off at twelve-thirty."

I remembered the blond guy making a phone call while I was waiting for my car, but I didn't mention it. "That's silly," I said. "Even if the bomb had been closer to the hotel it wouldn't have done any damage on the fifth floor."

"You haven't heard all of my theory yet," he said drily. "The rest of it goes like this. I think that bomb was in a box, probably cardboard, then wrapped in gift paper. Somebody received word of what time you'd probably be there, set the time and resealed the gift wrapping, then managed to have the gift placed in your room. I think you reached your room, saw the package and decided not to take any chances. You went to your balcony and threw it as far as you could toward the ocean."

"Wayne, you ought to take up writing. You have great imagination."

"Maybe," he grunted. "Do you remember me telling you that Angelo Bacci had two gunmen with him?"

"Yes."

"I forgot to tell you that one of them is not only a gunman. I thought it wasn't important at the time, but he is also an expert at bombs. That's what he did in World War Two, and he came out to use it for the Syndicate. The police know of several murders he committed that way in Chicago. They know it but could never prove it."

"The blond guy?"

"No. The other one. He's short and muscular with black hair. His name is Meyer Devlin."

"How'd he manage that combination?"

"His mother was German Jewish and his father Irish Catholic."

"Well," I said, "if Bacci is after me, I'll admit that this Devlin will probably be in on it. But I don't think they'd try to bomb me that way. A bomb under the hood of my car, maybe."

"Now," he said, his voice sounding harder, "I'll tell you a part that isn't theory. Shortly before you reached the hotel last night a man entered the hotel and said you were a friend of his. When told that you weren't there, he asked if they would put a package in your room. He said it was a present for you, and he gave a bellhop ten dollars to take it up and leave it in your room. The package was gift wrapped. Small pieces of colored wrapping paper were found on the beach in the vicinity of the spot where the bomb exploded."

"An interesting story," I said. "Someone did leave a present in my room for me last night. It was from someone I met on the plane when I came down. I don't think she would send a bomb. But if I find I need any protection from you, I'll let you know."

"Milo, you're a damn fool," he said harshly. He hung up.

I went back into the bar and sat down. Buck looked over at me. "You were gone a long time. It must've been a broad."

"Wrong, Buck. It was Lieutenant Dillman of Miami Beach's Finest. Like you, he seems to have the mistaken idea that I am connected with the bomb of last night."

"I hate to find myself in agreement with a cop, but I know what I think."

"And I know what I think. It's that you should serve me another drink."

He made a sound of disgust in his throat but poured the drink.

"Presently," I said, "I am going out to pursue the activities of my profession. If Miss Carlson should show up while I'm gone, tell her I will see her this evening."

"If you're able to get back," he murmured.

"I think there's a law against trying to bury someone before he's dead."

He grunted to himself and moved away, polishing the bar. I finished my drink and walked through the lobby to where I could look out the front door. The car was parked across the street with Carl Ketcher lounging behind the wheel and watching the front door. I got a bellhop to go outside and have one of the car-boys come into the lobby.

A moment later one of the boys came in. I told him to bring my Cadillac around and park in front of the lobby entrance, with the motor running, for five minutes, then take it back and park it. I could see he was a little curious about it, but five dollars took care of that.

I went back through the lobby, stopping to buy another newspaper at the newsstand, then went down to the side exit. A glance told me that Ketcher's attention was on my car and the front entrance. I lifted the newspaper so that it partly covered my face but looked as if I were reading it and walked out to a taxi parked on the side street. The driver opened the door and I climbed in. I took another look, but the blond was paying no attention to the cab. I told the driver to take me to the boat dock.

As we turned into Collins Avenue, I was still busy reading the newspaper. I didn't look back until we were half a block away. He was still waiting for me to come out of the hotel.

It was a short drive to the dock. I had the driver go slowly along the dock until I spotted the boat. We stopped there and I told the driver to wait for me. I walked down to the edge of the narrow pier. It was a trim-looking boat, probably large enough to sleep two.

"Ahoy, Aristotle," I called. "Anybody home?"

"Just a minute, mate," a voice answered.

I waited a moment and then he appeared from below. He was a stocky, muscular man with a pleasant, relaxed face and curly, gray-black hair. He looked to be about fifty, maybe a couple of years older.

"You selling something, mate?" he asked. His voice was friendly.

"Only myself," I said. "Are you Aristotle Murphy?"

"The same."

"Buck, the bartender at the Hapsburg Hotel, told me where to find you. I'd like to talk to you for a few minutes."

"Come aboard, lad."

I stepped onto the deck of the boat as he disappeared

70

below. I followed him. The interior was as neat as the outside. There was a single bed which folded up against the wall. There was also a small but adequate galley, a table and a couple of chairs, some book shelves filled with books. Soft music came from the radio on the table.

"What can I do for you, lad?"

"My name is Milo March. I work for an insurance company, and Buck is a friend of mine. I mentioned I wanted to find someone with a boat and he suggested I see you."

"Buck is a fine lad. We've had many a glass together. Where do you want to go?"

"No more than a few hundred yards," I said with a smile.

"Would you join me in a glass of grog now?" he asked. "I think better with a glass in my hand. Or is it too early for you?"

"I'll join you."

He brought two glasses and a big brown bottle. When he started pouring, I saw that it was rum. "You'll be wanting something with it?" he asked.

"No, thank you. I never try to improve on perfection."

"Aye, a good thought."

He finished pouring and shoved one glass across to me. I picked mine up and tasted it. It was good rum. I noticed that he was watching me without touching his own drink, but when I took a generous swallow after tasting it, he smiled and lifted his own glass.

"You can always tell a man," he said when he put his glass down, "by his liking for good liquor. What is your feeling about computers?"

"I'm opposed to them. I never saw a machine that I could have a drink with or with whom I'd want to climb in the sack, and I don't like being known as one-one-three—one-two—seven-six-seven-one."

There was an interested look on his face. "And who, in your opinion, is the greatest writer to have ever graced the English language?"

"Christopher Marlowe," I said promptly.

"And your favorite French poet?"

"Villon."

By this time his face was beaming. "A true rascal. I'll be glad to take you where you want to go. Where did you say it was?"

"I didn't say yet. You know where one Angelo Bacci lives?"

"Aye. He's part of the modern Sodom and Gomorrah. A friend of yours?"

"Hardly," I said. "I want to go up there twice. At night. Around at the back. The first time I merely want to take a good look. The second time I will want you to leave me there. I will pay you one hundred dollars for the two trips."

"It is too much money."

"Nevertheless, that's what I'll pay you. It's not my money. It's from the insurance company."

"The insurance company, eh? In that case, I'll take it. When do you want to go?"

"The first trip in the next day or two. I'm not sure about the second trip. I'll have to let you know."

"I'll be here."

I remembered what Buck had told me, and I took fifty

dollars from my pocket and put it on the table. "Half in advance and half after the second trip."

"Fair enough," he said. "Will you have another glass of grog?"

"Not today. I have too many things to do." I finished what was left in my glass.

"I was hoping," he said wistfully, "you could stop long enough for us to talk awhile. It isn't often I meet anyone who even heard of Marlowe or Villon."

"If I possibly can," I said, "I'll spend an evening with you before I leave Miami Beach." I started for the exit.

"Do that, lad," he called after me. "I'll look forward to it."

I went back to the taxi and gave the address of the mission home in Miami. I checked as we drove away, but there was no one following. We drove over the viaduct and a few minutes later were at the mission. Again I told the driver to wait and I went into the mission. I approached someone who looked like he belonged behind a desk.

"Pardon me," I said. "Could you tell me where I might find Speed Harris?"

He looked me over slowly before deciding on his answer. "He might be in the recreation room," he said pointing to an open doorway.

I entered the room. There were a couple of battered ping-pong tables, an equally battered television set and a table covered with magazines and pamphlets. There were seven or eight men in the room. All of them were listlessly watching television. There was only one man who looked small enough to have once been a jockey. I walked over to him.

"Speed Harris?" I asked.

He looked at me for a minute without answering. Then he nodded his head. "Fuzz?" he asked.

"No," I said. "Buck, the bartender at the Hapsburg, suggested that I see you. I'd like to talk to you for a few minutes. Where can we go?"

"We can talk in here. Nobody will pay any attention. They're too busy with the idiot box. There ain't anything else to do."

"I'd rather find a more private place. I'll buy coffee or a drink."

He licked his lips nervously. "A drink?" he asked.

"Sure. Where can we go?"

He was on his feet. "There's a bar a block down the street. I'll show you."

I followed him out to the street, stopping long enough to tell the cab driver to hold on and I'd be with him in a few minutes. Then we went on to the bar. It looked like hundreds of skid row bars all over the country. There were four helpless looking men nursing glasses of wine at the far end of the bar. Speed Harris and I took stools near the door. The bartender waddled up and looked at me.

"Give him a double shot of whatever he wants," I said, "and I'll have a shot of bourbon with a water chaser."

He went off and brought the drinks. I put out some money and waited until he'd given me the change and went back to his stool.

"My name is Milo March," I said then. "I work for an insurance company. Buck told me that you know a lot of the local hoods and fast-money boys."

"What if I do?" he asked. He looked at the pack of cigarettes I'd just taken from my pocket. "Got an extra butt?"

"Sure." I put the pack on the bar. "I'm looking for some information and I'll pay for it. Do you know Angelo Bacci?"

"Is this information for the cops?"

"No. It's for me."

He finished his drink and stared hungrily at the empty glass. I motioned to the bartender to refill it. I paid for it and waited for the bartender to leave. Then I waited some more.

"I used to know Bacci," he said finally, "when I was still riding. He used to be there every day. Whenever I rode a winner and he had money on it, he'd slip me a hundred or so. But I don't get out to the track much and he don't go to any of the bookie joints. But I do know some of the guys working for him."

"Do you think you could pick up any information for me?"

He'd had enough to drink to give him some courage, and he was thinking about the fact I'd said I would pay him. "Maybe I could. What kind of information? Most of them know me for so long that they talk in front of me as if I wasn't there."

"There are a few special things I want. Find out if an out-of-town hood came here to see Bacci about five or six weeks ago and where he came from. If possible find out his name. If you've heard any talk about bonds, or do hear any, I'd like to know that, too. Then just any general information you can pick up."

"You said you'd pay me? And you won't pass everything along to the local cops?"

"I'll pay you and I won't tell the local cops."

"How much?"

"I'll give you twenty dollars now." I took twenty from my pocket and gave it to him below the top of the bar. "If you dig up anything worthwhile, I'll give you another eighty dollars."

He had slipped the twenty into his pocket. "Boy, can I use this. I put everything I had yesterday on a sure-thing round-robin. Only the second horse started his run too late and lost by a nose. Another ten feet and he would've been in." He paused and then said, "I can tell you the first thing now if you'll give me another five bucks."

"Okay." I took a five from my pocket and passed it to him.

"It's more like four weeks ago," he said. "Some guy was here from Chicago. I think he only stayed a couple of days. But he was in the bookie joint one day with two of Bacci's guns. I didn't hear his name though. Maybe I can find it out."

"Try," I said. "There's one more thing I'd like you to try to get."

"What?"

"Anything about that girl who was killed in the Everglades a little more than a week ago."

"I . . . I can't ask any questions. You understand that. But if I hear anything I'll let you know."

"Okay. I'll drop back to see you in a couple of days. If you want to get in touch with me before that, call the Hapsburg Hotel in Miami Beach and ask for Milo March." I took a dollar from my pocket and placed it on the bar in front of him. "Have another drink on me. I'll see you soon."

He nodded and I left. I told the cab driver to head back for the Beach. We had almost reached it when I remembered something else.

"Driver," I said, "do you know where there's a gun store? I want to buy a gun."

He gave me a startled look in the rear-view mirror.

"Don't push the panic button," I told him. "I have a Florida gun permit and I'll register the gun as soon as I get it."

He didn't say anything, but he did drive me straight to a gun store. I showed my permit, gave the salesman my address and told him what I wanted. He brought out several .25 caliber automatics. They aren't very good except at close range and then only if you can put the bullet where you want it. But they fit other requirements which I had. I picked one out and bought it. I also bought a belt holster for it and some ammunition.

Then I had the driver take me to the police station, where I registered it. Then back to the hotel. Ketcher, the blond gunman, was still parked out front. I managed to get into the side entrance without being spotted by him. I went straight up to my room. After loading the clip, I put it into the automatic and dropped it into a dresser drawer. I decided to push a little more. I addressed three manila envelopes, put a photograph of the dead girl in each one and went downstairs to mail them.

The clerk gave me a telegram. It was a Western Union money order for a thousand dollars from Intercontinental Insurance. I signed it and asked the clerk if he'd cash it and put the money in the safe until I needed it.

"Certainly, Mr. March," he said. "You had one phone

call. From room five-twenty." That was Betty Carlson's room. I thanked the clerk and went into the bar. Buck came over.

"Where have you been?" he asked.

"I looked up Speed Harris and your friend Aristotle Murphy."

"What did you think of him?"

"Quite a character is Aristotle. I made arrangements with him and promised him I'd try to come down for a social evening before I left town. Speed Harris is going to try to get some information for me. Do I have to give a full report before I can get a drink?"

"VO?" he asked.

I nodded and he brought me the drink. "Betty Carlson called to see if you were here."

"She left a message for me at the desk. I'll call her in a few minutes."

I sipped my drink and listened to Buck talk about the various tenants in the hotel. Finally it was one o'clock in the afternoon. I went over to the house phone and called Betty Carlson."

"Milo March," I said when she answered. "How do you feel today?"

"I think I'm recovered," she said with a laugh. "What have you been doing?"

"Working. Dinner tonight?"

"I'd love it."

"Good. Meet me in the bar about five o'clock."

"I'll be there, Milo."

I said goodbye, and then put in a call to Lieutenant Dillman. He answered right away.

"Milo March," I said.

"Nice of you to call. Did you finally decide to give a little cooperation?"

"I always cooperate. You know that, Wayne. What you were asking for wouldn't do you any good. Suppose I had said that I thought the bomb was meant for me and that I thought it was part of the case. What could you do with it? Sure, you could ask questions, but you wouldn't learn enough to make an arrest. In the meantime you'd tip them off to the fact that I am cooperating with you, so they'd be more careful the next time they tried to get me. I don't want them to be more careful. I want them to be careless."

"I guess you're right, Milo. I was just hoping that you had something that would enable us to move in on them."

"I don't. I have a lot of ideas which are probably right. I think I'm making progress, but we're still a long way from arrests, let alone a trial. Do you keep track of out-of-town hoods who visit Miami Beach?"

"We try to. I don't work on that, but we have a department that does. Why?"

"There was a hood here from Chicago about four weeks ago. He was around for only two days but was seen with those two hoods of Bacci's. I don't know his name or who he works for. I'd like to know both things."

"I'll check it out."

"One more thing, Wayne. Check with the phone company and see if Bacci made any phone calls to Chicago just prior to the visit from the hood."

"I'll get back to you. Where are you? The hotel?"

"Yeah. I'll wait to hear from you." I hung up and went

back to the bar. "Let me have one more, Buck. Then I'll have some lunch."

"Okay." He went over and reached for the bottle. He stopped and looked at me. "If you're having lunch, you want the VO or a martini?"

"You're right, Buck. Let's have a martini."

Just as I finished the drink, the operator paged me over the loudspeaker system. I went to the house phone and took the call there.

"Milo," he said. It was Dillman. "Got it. The Chicago man was Roberto Granetti. He's a well-known hood in Chicago. Works as a chauffeur and gunman for Angelo Benotti, one of the wheels in the Syndicate there. Want me to check them out with the Chicago police?"

"No need to. I know both of them. What about the phone calls?"

"Angelo Bacci made two phone calls to Chicago about that time. Both were to Benotti. Think I should follow up on that?"

"No," I said. "There isn't anything you can do to them, and you won't learn anything that will let you grab. Besides, I know Benotti and I may be able to find out what I need to know. You, or any other cop, would just louse it up."

"Thanks a lot," he said drily. "If the captain wants to know anything, I'll just tell him I'm waiting to hear from you. Keep in touch, Milo."

"Will do," I said, and hung up. I walked out to the patio and took a small table where I had a good view of the pool and the sun bathers. It was a stimulating view.

The waitress came over and I ordered another martini. I also ordered pompano. It's a local fish and, when cooked right, will make you think you never heard of fish before.

I leaned back and thought about the case. It was interesting that Benotti and Granetti were involved. I did know both of them. And they knew me, but not as Milo March. As Peter Miloff. I had been recalled by the Army to do a job for the CIA. It was to go to Russia to help them plan and build vending machines. The CIA made a deal with Benotti, who'd been asked by the Russians to lend them a vending machine expert. Like all gangsters and hoods, Benotti thought of himself as an American patriot who loved his country. He got in touch with someone in the government.

The CIA talked to Benotti. He easily agreed to help them. The help was to present me as one of his men and to let them hire me, subject to the approval of the State Department. The approval was granted with unseemly haste. Benotti provided me with a background and proof that I worked for him. Roberto Granetti taught me about vending machines. Both of them had been very friendly, even though they knew I was a government agent. Now it might come in handy.

After lunch I went up to my room, undressed and got into bed. I was tense, but I managed to relax enough to go to sleep.

I was awake by four o'clock. I showered and shaved and got dressed. I debated calling Benotti but decided to put it off until the next day. I went down to the bar.

Betty Carlson arrived promptly at five. She looked great. We had a couple of drinks at the bar, and then I suggested that we have dinner in the hotel. I thought she might object, but I was a little afraid to take a girl out now that the pressure was building up. When I suggested it, however, she seemed happy about the idea.

We went into the largest of the five restaurants and the only one with entertainment. We had a couple more drinks there and then ordered dinner. Afterwards we watched the show while having coffee and brandy. Betty was getting a little high, but just enough to be more relaxed.

It was eleven o'clock when the first show was over. "Would you like to go back to the bar?" I asked her. "I know this isn't a very exciting evening but I'll make it up to you."

"Oh, I'm enjoying myself. And I haven't found anyone to really talk to since I've been here. I'd love to talk some more, if it won't be too dull for you, and I haven't liked being alone since that terrible explosion last night. Did you hear it?"

"I read about it this morning. I don't think it's anything to worry about. What do you want to do?"

"Why don't we go up to my room and have a couple of drinks and talk? Then I'll send you home. I don't want to drink too much tonight. I ought to have at least a couple of days between hangovers."

"Your room's in the front of the building, isn't it?"

"Yes."

"I've got a better idea," I said. "My room is in the back, and there's a balcony overlooking the ocean. Why don't we go there, and then you can leave whenever you want to."

"All right," she said.

We went up to my room and I led her out to the balcony. "What would you like to drink?" I asked her.

"I think a Tom Collins."

I went inside and phoned room service. I told them to send up a double Collins in a tall glass and a bucket of ice. Then I opened the closet door so that it would screen me and took off my jacket and hung it up. Then I removed the shoulder holster and put it and the gun up on the shelf. I went into the bathroom and fooled around until I heard the knock on the door. I let the waiter in and signed the check. I carried the drink, the ice and my bottle of VO out to the balcony.

"It's so beautiful out here," she said, "that I wish I'd thought of asking for one when I came here."

"They'll probably let you exchange rooms. I don't think they're that busy this time of year."

I sat down next to her and we talked. Or, rather, she talked. Not about anything important. She merely sounded lonely. I don't know how long she kept it up, but then she suddenly stopped in that mysterious way that such things sometimes happen. The next minute she was in my arms. I put my hand on her chin and gently lifted her face and kissed her.

At first, I thought she was going to pull away, then she was pressing her lips to mine and her whole body was trembling. When the kiss ended, I took her hand. We both stood up and I led her inside. She was trembling so badly I had to help her undress. Then I undressed while she stared at me with her big brown eyes. I stretched out beside her and took her in my arms. She came to me with a little sighing noise deep in her throat.

Later, I was lying beside her, my left arm around her shoulders. With my right hand I was stroking her body gently. My fingers passed down over her flat stomach, then suddenly encountered something that made me stop. I lifted my head and looked.

There, just below her navel, was a crescent-shaped scar.

6

A few minutes passed before it completely soaked in. At first I knew what it was and I didn't. Then the full realization came to me. It was the scar that was described in the flyer on Jane Carlton, the second of the two girls. I doubted if there were many people with crescent-shaped scars on their bodies. There were probably less who had such a scar in that exact spot. In fact, I would have been willing to bet there were no others.

"Milo," she said, "is there something wrong?"

"Nothing wrong, honey," I said. "I was just seeing for the first time how beautiful you are."

"I . . . I thought you were looking at my scar."

"I noticed it but didn't pay any attention. I think that everyone has scars if you look close enough."

"I fell on some broken glass when I was a teen-ager. It hurt a lot at the time, but then I forgot about it until I got older."

"Forget about it. Or think of it as a beauty mark." I patted the scar. "I'm going to have another drink. Want one?"

"Please."

I went to the glass door that opened onto the balcony. I looked out but there was nobody on the other balconies. I stepped outside and picked up the bottle, the bucket of ice and the glasses and went back into the room. I put everything down on the night table. "You want the same thing, Betty?"

"I'll have whatever you're having."

I poured two glasses of VO, only mine was on the rocks and I added water to hers. Then I lit two cigarettes and handed one to her. I got into bed and raised my glass.

"You know," I said, "I think maybe these college kids today have something. Here's to love."

"You're not in love with me," she said.

"I didn't say I was, but we just got through making love. I suspect that making love is one of the ways to find one kind of love."

"I wouldn't know," she said, and there was a sad note in her voice.

After that she didn't seem too interested in talking. I turned on television and we watched a late movie. It was still on when I became aware that she had fallen asleep. I got up and covered her, then climbed back into bed and watched the rest of the movie. When it was over I turned the set off, snapped off the light and returned to bed.

I was thinking about the crescent-shaped scar when I fell asleep.

I was up early the next morning. She was still asleep. I looked down at her. In repose, her face looked like that of a little girl. I thought what prison would do to someone like her. She might be able to avoid it and be put on probation if she would listen to me. But it was too early to bring it up. I'd have to wait a day or two. I poured a straight shot of VO for myself and turned the television on for the Today Show. I lit a cigarette and went back to bed with my drink.

Sometime later she awakened. I felt her move and glanced at her. Her eyes were open, staring straight up at the ceiling. Her face was filled with fear. I watched her without saying anything.

Finally, with an obvious effort, she turned her head to look at me. Slowly, some of the fear began to fade.

"Good morning," I said.

"Why didn't you wake me up?" she asked. "I didn't mean to stay here all night."

"Why should I bother you? You were sleeping peacefully so I let you continue. Would you like some breakfast?"

"Here?"

"Why not?"

"Oh, no, I couldn't," she said. "I don't want the waiter to see me here. Everybody in the hotel would know about it."

"Nobody would know and nobody would care. What do you think people do here? Play solitaire?"

"No," she said, shaking her head. "I must go back to my room." She swung her legs out of the bed and almost ran to the bathroom, grabbing up her clothes as she went. I stayed where I was.

When she came out she was fully dressed. She stood there looking at me for a minute, then came over and kissed me lightly. "Will I see you again?" she asked.

"Sure," I said. "I'll probably see you tonight, but it may not be in time for dinner. I might have to do some work."

"At night? I thought you said you worked for an insurance company."

"I do. We're a big company with offices all over the world. I'm what might be called a trouble-shooter, so that means I quite often have to work at night."

"All right. Thank you, Milo."

"For what?"

"For being gentle." She went to the door, opened it and peered out. Then she was swiftly gone.

I checked the bottle. There was still three or four drinks in it. I called room service and ordered my breakfast and a bucket of ice. I unlocked the door and got my gun from the closet shelf and went back to bed.

When the knock came I called for him to come in and waited to see if it were the waiter. It was. He pushed the table over to the bed. I signed the check and he went away.

I had another drink on the rocks. By that time I was fully awake, so I had breakfast. I showered, shaved and got dressed, then sat down to think for a minute.

Bacci and his friends were already pretty well stirred up, but I thought I'd push it a little farther and I'd have to make additional preparations. I went down to the drugstore on the level below the lobby. I bought a roll of adhesive tape and returned to my room. I took the automatic holster from the drawer and taped it to my left leg just above the ankle. I put the loaded clip in the gun and then slipped it into the holster. I stood up and took a look. It didn't show. I went downstairs, picked up a morning paper in the lobby and then went on into the bar.

Buck brought over a VO and water. "How did your date go last night?"

"Fine."

"I hear you went upstairs pretty early last night."

"You know how it is, Buck. When you're working hard you have to get your sleep."

"Not the way you work."

"You don't understand, Buck," I said patiently. "Did you ever see a woman shopping in a store for fresh peaches?"

"Yeah, but what's that got to do with it?"

"Everything. I work the way that woman shops. I go around giving a little pinch to all the peaches and pretty soon I've found all the ones I'm looking for. Then I put them in a box and close the lid."

"It's a hell of a way to catch anything except a peach —or maybe a broad."

"It works," I said cheerfully.

"Maybe," he grunted. "Who you going to pinch today?"

"The same ones. When they're bruised enough then the case will be over."

"Okay, okay. I know when I'm being told to mind my own business."

I stayed with the one drink until it was almost noon. Then I went out to the lobby and looked through the front door. The car was there all right, but there were two men in it instead of one. The blond was still behind the wheel. The other man was dark-haired and just as mean looking. This probably meant it was M-Day—for March Day. I stepped out front and asked one of the boys to bring my car around.

While I waited, I pretended to not even be aware of the car, but I still kept it in view enough to catch any sudden move from it. I felt a little the way a rabbit must feel when he sees the hunter lift his gun. I think scared is the word.

The Cadillac pulled up in front of the hotel entrance and the boy got out. I thanked him with legal tender and slipped behind the wheel. I pulled onto Collins Avenue and drove north. The other car fell in behind me.

After several miles, they still hadn't shown any desire to do more than keep pace, so I gave a little more attention to where I was going.

It wasn't long before I reached Hollywood. I stopped in at a gas station and asked directions. The car behind continued to follow like an obedient poodle.

Tony Antonio lived in a house near the ocean. It was a house almost as big as Bacci's house. Almost but not quite. It was what you would expect from someone of slightly lower rank. I parked in front of it and went up to ring the doorbell. I noticed the other car had parked about a block behind me.

The door opened. The man who stood there didn't look like a servant. He also didn't look like anyone who would be the owner of the house. I noticed that he was carrying a gun beneath his jacket.

"I'd like to see Tony Antonio," I said.

"Who are you?"

"My name is Milo March."

A look of recognition rolled over his face. "Yeah, I've heard of you. Come on in."

"Thank you," I said. I stepped past him and waited.

The door closed behind me. "Go ahead," he said. "It's the first door on the right."

I walked into a huge living room, tastefully furnished. I spotted the door on the right and walked up to it. It was closed.

"Knock on the door," the voice from behind me said. I knocked.

"Come in," a voice called from the room.

I opened the door and stepped in to what looked like a game room—but there weren't any games. There were only two immense couches, four or five chairs, small side tables, a television set and a desk with a man sitting behind it. He had to be Tony Antonio. He had dark olive skin and deep black hair and a beard that probably always looked as if he needed a shave. His clothes were expensive sport items, and most people would probably have said he was handsome—unless they looked closer at his eyes and face. There was an expression of surprise on his face for just a second, then his gaze shifted to a spot behind me.

"This is Milo March," my escort said. "He wanted to see you."

"That is," I cut in, "if you're Tony Antonio."

His eyes focused on me again. "I'm Tony Antonio. Come on in and sit down." He waited until I sat in the chair in front of his desk. "This is Dan Hackett. He's my secretary."

"I guessed as much," I said. "I noticed he was carrying his eraser."

I thought it was a pretty funny line, but nobody even smiled. Antonio stared at me for a second, then his gaze shifted toward the door. "You can go, Dan. I won't need you."

We both waited to hear the door close. When it did, he turned back to me. "I've heard of you, Mr. March. Are you the one who's been sending me photographs of a dead girl? If so, is it some kind of joke?"

"I may have sent it," I said. "I send so many things to so many people I really can't keep track of all of them. But if I did, it's no joke. I don't play practical jokes."

"And I don't like jokes," he said. "I don't know anything about that broad and I never saw her in my life."

"Now you've seen her in your life," I said, "but not in her life. Well, if you don't know anything about her, what do you know about some bonds and securities that were boosted recently in New York?"

"I don't know a damn thing about bonds or securities," he said. He was beginning to sound angry—which was the way I wanted him. "What right do you have to ask questions? You some kind of an insurance cop?"

"I'm some kind of insurance investigator. It's a slightly more dignified word. You're Angelo Bacci's partner, aren't you?"

"Angelo is my friend and we do own a couple of businesses together. But we are not partners."

"Do you know a man named Jack Daly?"

"I've met him, but I wouldn't say I know him well."

"What about Bobby Dixon?" I asked.

"I think I met him once or twice. Purely social."

"Sure it was. And you don't know anything about bonds and securities, huh? I have a different version of it. Jack Daly and Bobby Dixon got two square broads in New York to dip their fingers into the till for one and a half million dollars. The two guys and at least one of the broads came down here. They finally sold the bonds and securities to you and Angelo Bacci—at a good discount, I'm sure. Daly and Dixon probably slipped the broads a few grand and put the rest in their pockets. Then they began to worry about the fact that the two broads could testify against them. I suspect you and Bacci worried a little, too. So they killed one of the two broads, maybe both of them. If it were both, that probably makes you and Bacci feel a little safer. But not enough. When are you going to hit Daly and Dixon?"

His face had gotten darker as I talked, and his mouth had slowly tightened. He reached over and pushed a button on his desk. I knew what to expect. The door behind me opened.

"Yes, boss?" It was Hackett's voice.

"Mr. March is leaving," Antonio said tightly. "When he gets outside, be sure that you lock the door so he can't sneak back in."

"Yes, boss. It'll be a pleasure. Come on punk."

"Talking to yourself, Hackett?" I asked as I stood up. I looked back at my involuntary host. "I'll see you around, Antonio."

He didn't answer but just stared at me as if he were a tailor measuring me for a suit. My last suit. I walked past Hackett to the front door and opened it. I stepped outside and turned to look at him.

"Take it easy, Hackett. This looks like a neighborhood

with class. Not a slum. It might upset the neighbors if they saw me kill you."

"Get out," he said. "I'll catch up with you soon."

"I am out, Hackett. I hope you do catch up with me. I think a bullet might do a lot to improve your appearance." I turned and walked to the Cadillac. As I drove off, I saw the other car pull away from the curb and follow.

When I reached the main drag, I turned left and headed back for Miami Beach. It was shortly after noon and there was little traffic on the road. Finally there was a stretch where the only cars in sight were mine and that of the two hoods following me. Glancing in the rear-view mirror, I saw that they had picked up speed and were gaining on me.

"Milo, my boy," I said aloud, "I think there's going to be a little action. Now you start earning your money."

I slipped my gun from the shoulder holster, triggered off the safety and held it in my lap. The window on my left was already down. I drove with my left hand and kept my right on the gun.

A moment later, the other car was pulling up beside me as if passing. I knew better, but I didn't look around until it was almost in position. Then I turned my head to look.

The black-haired man was just bringing his gun into sight.

7

There wasn't much time. I took a fast glance at the road ahead of me, then turned my head, lifted the gun and shot twice, as fast as I could pull the trigger. At the same time I stepped on the brakes. The last glimpse I had of the dark-haired man, he was sliding down on the seat. I wasn't really sure whether I'd hit him or if he were sliding to safety.

I brought the car to a halt and glanced in the rear-view mirror. There were no cars in sight behind me. I looked ahead. The other car had also stopped. Ketcher, the driver, had just opened the door on his side and had one foot on the ground. I shifted the Cadillac into drive and stepped on the gas. The Cadillac plowed into the back of his car. His door swung back and hit him and I saw him starting to fall out.

I backed up quickly, put it into drive again and pulled around him while he was still rolling on the ground. I gunned my car and kept my foot down on the accelerator until I was out of sight. I kept the speed up and watched the rear-view mirror, but the other car didn't show up.

There was still nobody behind me when I reached the hotel. I turned the car over to the boy and went inside. I checked with the desk. They said I'd had one call, but the person hadn't left his name. I went on into the bar. Buck brought over a drink.

"How's it going?" he asked.

"Mostly in low gear," I said. "You know how it is."

"As a matter of fact, I'm glad I don't know how it is. I wouldn't be able to sleep tonight."

"Look how much you miss by sleeping so much."

"Yeah," he said and moved away to serve another customer.

I tossed off the drink to calm my nerves, then went upstairs. I removed the two empty shells from my gun and put in two fresh ones. Then I cleaned the gun very carefully and replaced it in the holster. I went back downstairs, stopping at the desk for a handful of change.

In the phone booth, I looked up the phone number of Jack Daly. I dialed it.

"Mr. Daly?" I asked when a man answered.

"He ain't here right now. Who's calling?"

"First," I said, "who's answering the phone?"

"I live here, too," he said. "I'm Bobby Dixon. You want to leave a message for Jack?"

"I do," I said. "You may have heard of me. My name is Milo March. I . . . ."

He interrupted to tell me what he thought of me. It wasn't worth repeating, but it did give me a general idea of his thinking—and his vocabulary. He continued until he ran out of breath.

"I didn't know you were educated," I said when he

finally stopped. "I guess I never realized that men's rooms had such a rounded curriculum. I just wanted to tell you boys it's about time for you to find out where you can retreat under a rock. Your friends aren't doing so good. They've tried to kill me twice and didn't make it. The second time, which was today, they got hurt. If they can't protect you, who will? You boys might be able to kill a girl, but you'll never make it in the big league. Your petticoats would start showing before you reached first base."

He started to repeat what he'd said before, but I hung up on him. I looked up Bacci but decided not to call him. I dialed Daly's number again.

"This is March," I said when Dixon answered. "If you talk to Bacci, tell him that I suggest he take a long vacation in Sicily. The dam is about to break." I hung up before he could answer.

Next, I dialed the operator and asked her if she could find the number of an Angelo Benotti in Chicago and place a call to him. She wanted me to dial Information myself, but I told her I had bad vision and talked her into doing it herself. She found the number and a moment later had the call through. A man answered the phone.

"I'd like to speak to Angelo Benotti," I said.

"Who's calling?" the man asked.

"Tell him it's Peter Miloff," I said.

"Peter," he said, coming on the phone, "is that really you?"

"It's really me, Angelo. How are you?"

"Fine, fine. I was hoping I might hear from you some day. I understand that the last position worked out okay."

97

"It wasn't the last one," I said, "but it worked out fine. I would have called you, but I've been too busy. I wanted to tell you how grateful I was for your help."

"I was glad to do it," he said. "It was a real pleasure to do something for the country that's been so wonderful to me." That was typical of most of the hoods I'd met. Strictly cornball about the country whose laws they were always breaking. "What can I do for you, Peter?"

"I was hoping I could do something for you."

"What do you mean?" His voice had taken on a new quality. He automatically started playing it close to his chest.

"I'm working on a new assignment," I said carefully. "It starts in Florida and where it goes after that I don't know. But I accidentally ran into something which I think might concern you. You helped me and I feel that I owe you something. That's all there is to it."

"I really appreciate that," he said. I could tell again by his voice that he was trying to be careful and was hoping I would be the same. He probably always had the idea that his phone might be tapped. It probably was.

"Well," I said, being equally careful, "this is not your vending machine business, but I remembered that you were always interested in the stock market, and it does concern that. You might just call it a market tip on some blue-ribbon securities. It's the least I can do for you at the moment."

"It's great of you," he said. I could sense that he was being more relaxed. "What is it, Peter?"

"I understand that a mutual friend of ours was here recently. At least it sounded like him. I believe he was probably arranging a shipment of goods which could change the price on Wall Street of certain securities. It also sounds as if it were the kind of change that would indicate a need to sell at an early date."

"Is the mutual friend the one you spent a vacation with?"

"I think so."

He laughed. "I really appreciate this call, Peter. I do know about it, and you're right. It is going to force the price up for a short time, but they do have to be sold quickly. It's always better to take a sure but quick profit than to wait until the market falls out from under you. Our mutual friend is leaving tonight and will be in Boston tomorrow to confirm the deal. I knew about the time element but I still owe you something."

"Not a thing, Angelo."

"The first time you're in Chicago, call me and we'll have dinner together. When are you leaving Florida and where are you going?"

"Probably soon and I don't know where. Probably south. I'll call you whenever I get there. And say hello to our friend."

"I will. Take care of yourself, Peter. You have given me a breath of fresh air. You are truly my brother. And, again, thanks."

He hung up. I leaned back in the phone booth and took a deep breath. It had worked.

There was one more phone call to make. I thought about it a minute, then put in a person-to-person call to Lieutenant John Rockland, New York City Police Department. It took a few minutes but finally I heard his voice.

"Hello, Johnny," I said. "Milo March."

"I should have guessed," he said wearily. "What do you want this time?"

"I want to do you a favor," I said.

"Give it to me gently. I don't want to get a heart attack."

"Know anybody in the Boston fuzz?"

"I might. You want to turn Boston around, too?"

"No. I've got a plum for you this time. You know the case I'm working on?"

"Yeah. What about it?"

"Want to recover the bonds and securities?"

"How?"

"There's a guy named Roberto Granetti in Chicago. He was here recently and took the goods back to Chicago. He'll be in Boston tomorrow morning with the goods. Boston must have pictures and a description on this guy, so they can spot him when he gets off the plane. Find out the flights and meet everyone until they see him. If I were them, I'd follow him and see who he turns them over to and then bust the whole bunch."

"Yes, sir, Chief. Anything else, Chief?"

Somehow I felt he wasn't showing the proper respect, since I was handing him a real prize, and I told him what he could do.

"Watch it, boy," he said. "You're talking to a police official and there's a law against language like that. Anyway, thanks, Milo. If it works out, I'll forgive you for all those other calls you made to me. I'll let you know how it turns out. Will you still be down there?"

"I think so. The Hapsburg hotel—or the nearest hospital or morgue. Take care, Johnny."

I replaced the receiver and picked up the rest of my

change. I went back upstairs and called room service. I ordered a bottle of VO, some ice cubes and lunch. Hanging up my jacket, I sat down and waited. Just as the doorbell rang, I realized that I was still wearing the gun. I unbuckled it and tossed it into the closet, then let the waiter in.

When he was gone, I made a drink and was ready to have my lunch. I had just finished when there was a knock on the door. I went over to it. "Who is it?" I asked.

"Wayne Dillman," he said.

I opened the door and the lieutenant came in. "Is this the way you work?" He asked.

"You know a better way?" I asked. "May I offer you a drink, or is that against regulations?"

"Technically, I'm not on duty so I'll have one."

I made him a drink with water and poured myself one on the rocks. I handed him his glass and he sat down in the chair.

"How are things going?" he asked.

"Creeping along," I said cheerfully. "I think things are getting a little tighter. You know how it is. A crack shows up here and then there, and pretty soon the dam collapses."

"Yeah. I know. What did you do today? Besides sitting at the bar or in your room?"

"I didn't do much but I think I accomplished something. I drove up and paid a social call on one of the state's outstanding citizens."

"Anybody I know?"

"You might know him. His name is Tony Antonio."

"I've heard of him," he said drily. "Did he serve tea and cookies?"

"Come to think of it, he didn't. It wasn't very polite of him. Actually, his butler wasn't too polite either."

"Dan Hackett?"

"I think that was his name. Pleasant sort of chap, but it didn't seem that he knew his business too well."

"What did you do out there?"

"Talked. Antonio didn't contribute much to the conversation, but I think he was shaken up. That was all I was trying to do."

"When did you come back?"

"Shortly after noon."

"Anything interesting happen on the trip?"

"It was quiet. Very little traffic. It was a breeze."

"I'm sure it was. I had an interesting day, too. Remember the bomb that went off outside the hotel?"

"Sure. What about it? Don't tell me that another one went off?"

"Not exactly the same. Do you also remember that I told you one of Bacci's gunmen was an expert in bombs?"

"I think you did mention it."

"Do you remember that I told you the name of that hood?"

"I think you did," I said, "but I don't remember it. I think it was an unusual name."

"It was Meyer Devlin. Today, he and Carl Ketcher just happened to be out of town. Shortly after noon, Meyer Devlin was found in a ditch beside the road between here and Hollywood. He was dead. There was a bullet in his head. It was a thirty-eight."

"I'm sorry to hear that. A gang war?"

"You don't know anything about it?"

"Me?" I asked in surprise. "Why should I know anything about it?"

"Let's stop playing games, Milo," he said wearily. "I think that Devlin and Ketcher tried to kill you on the way back to Miami Beach and that you killed Devlin and got away. You carry a .38. Where is it?"

"In the closet. Help yourself."

He walked over and opened the closet door. He pulled out the holster and took the gun from it. First, he smelled the barrel, then checked the bullets. Then he put it back in the closet.

"Seems to me," he said, "that you just cleaned the gun."

"I always take good care of my guns," I said gravely.

"Yeah. Of course, I could check it through ballistics, but I don't suppose you'd really have anything to do with killing Devlin."

"Me?" I said in a surprised tone. "I wouldn't do anything like that."

"Of course not. It also came to my attention that you bought and registered another gun since you've been here."

"Sure," I said. "But it's only a .25. Want to look at it?" I pulled up the leg of my pants, took the gun from the holster and handed it to him. "It's never even been fired. I just liked the looks of it and bought it. I registered it and my Florida license is still good.

He took the gun and examined it. "I know about the license. I checked it before I came up here. You know, you have to shoot pretty straight with this if you expect to do more than dent the wall."

"I shoot pretty straight when I have to," I said.

"What's the idea of all this? You suddenly become a gun fancier?"

"I just like to keep up with what's going on," he said. "But I don't get much cooperation."

"The only thing I can cooperate about," I said, "is not in your jurisdiction. That involves something I know. What concerns you is things I'm guessing. I'll tell you about them, too—if you don't go charging in like a bull in a china shop."

"I'll listen," he said.

"Okay. The bonds and securities were here a few weeks ago. Somebody from Chicago picked them up and took them back there. They are now on their way to Boston and I expect that the Boston police will pick them up there."

"Who had them here?"

"I can't prove it and I doubt if you can, but it was Bacci. I'd consider it a favor if you didn't lean on him until I'm through with him. I can use methods that you can't."

"Like killing Devlin?"

"I didn't even know Devlin," I said. "I wouldn't say that I'm all shaken up about him, but I'm not in the habit of killing people and throwing them in ditches."

"Okay," he said. "I'll give you enough rope to hang yourself. Incidentally, don't get the idea that Bacci will be shorthanded because of Devlin. He's already been replaced."

"The prince is dead, long live the prince. Who is it?"

"Hackett moved down about an hour ago. Antonio has a new gun coming down from Fort Lauderdale. I'll have a report on him later this afternoon." He stood up. "Take care of yourself."

"I always do. I'm the only me I've got. I'll see you around."

"You'd better," he said. "Thanks for the drink." He left.

I finished my drink and put the glass on the table. The phone rang. I picked up the receiver and said hello.

"This is the guy you bought some drinks for the other day over in Miami," he said. "Remember?"

"I remember."

"I think I got something for you. I don't want to talk about it on the phone. You want to come over and see me?"

"Okay," I said. "I'll meet you at that bar where we had the drinks." I glanced at my watch. "Five o'clock. Is that okay?"

"Okay," he said and hung up.

I stretched out on the bed and went to sleep. It was liable to be a long night.

At four-thirty I was awake. I washed the sleep out of my eyes, buckled on the holster and slipped into my jacket. Then I went downstairs. I stopped in at the bar for one drink.

"Where you been?" Buck asked.

"Getting my beauty sleep."

"Some guys have all the luck. Hear the news?"

"No. I haven't read Dick Tracy today. What happened?"

"A guy got knocked off. Meyer Devlin. He was a gun for that Angelo Bacci."

"My, my," I said. "All this violence upsets me. I'll see you later, Buck."

I went through the lobby and looked out the front door. To my surprise, the usual car wasn't across the street. Maybe Ketcher was home mourning his late friend. I had a boy bring the Cadillac around and I headed for Miami.

It was a few minutes after five when I reached the street where the mission was located. I drove past it towards the bar. There were a bunch of people gathered on the sidewalk in front of it. Several were obviously winos, while the others looked like they might live in the neighborhood. I parked and walked to the bar. I noticed the glass window was broken. I decided there must have been a fight.

I made my way through the crowd and entered the bar. There were a few drinkers who weren't to be distracted by anything. The same bartender was working and he came over to me. I ordered bourbon and water backed.

"Have a little trouble in here?" I asked when he brought the drink.

"Not in here," he said. "Outside on the street."

"A fight?"

"Don't reckon you could rightly call it a fight. A car drove by and a man was shot as he was starting to come in here. Killed him. And drove away.

"Anybody see it?" I asked curiously.

He shook his head. "Don't guess so. Nobody said they did. The cops was here, but they didn't seem to get anything except the name of the man who was killed."

"Somebody from around here?"

"Yes. Used to be a pretty good jockey. Maybe you heard of him. Speed Harris. Was big in his time, but the last few years he was just a guy on the juice. Don't figure why anybody would want to kill him." He stopped and took a closer look at me. "Say, ain't you the guy who was in here with Speed a couple of days ago?"

"I was here with him," I said wearily. "Does anybody have an idea who killed him or why?"

"If they do, they ain't saying. The only thing I heard was that it was a big black car with two men in it. Nobody got a good look at them or at the license plate—or, if they did, they ain't saying anything. Can't blame them much. Were you a friend of Speed's?"

"Not exactly," I said. I thought I should make a better explanation than that. "I used to know him when he was riding. Somebody told me he was down on his luck and living at the mission down the street. I looked him up and gave him some money."

"I figured you did," he said. "I know he had a few bucks the last couple of days. Also said he hit a horse and I knew he didn't have the bread for a bet before you was here. He was a nice little guy. Can't figure why anybody would kill him. Unless it was for something he knew from before. When he was riding winners, a lot of hoods used to pay a lot of attention to him and hang around him. Maybe it was something that went back to that."

"Maybe," I said. But I knew better. He must have made a mistake by asking too many questions. So for the promise of a hundred dollars I had bought his life. It made me feel just great.

"I was supposed to meet him today," I said slowly. "I was going to give him some more money."

"Well," he said, "I guess the only way you can see him today is if you go to the morgue. But maybe he's better off, mister. You ever think about that?"

"What do you mean?"

"If you're a guy who's used to being a winner—and Speed certainly was—when the day comes that you're no longer a winner, maybe it's too much. Maybe you can't go out in the park and pitch horseshoes after pitching horses all your life. In his case, horses were the only thing he knew. Maybe if he'd thought about it earlier he could have gone on to be a trainer or something of the sort and been happy. But he didn't think about it. Then, suddenly, he wasn't a winner anymore. He couldn't even get a mount. There was nothing left for him except booze and trying to get two bucks to bet on a horse. He didn't even care if he won. Betting on a horse was the nearest he could get to one. So maybe he's better off dead. . . . Probably killed by a horse player who once tipped him."

It was a long speech for that guy. It made sense. "You're right," I said. I finished my drink. "Thank you. You've already made me feel better. Did he have any family?"

"Only horses."

"What about the arrangements?"

He shrugged. "I guess the mission will bury him. We'll take up a collection here for flowers. It won't be much because nobody has any dough around here. But everybody here liked Speed and will do what they can."

"I have an idea," I said. I reached in my pocket and pulled out my money. I took out a fifty dollar bill and put it on the bar. "I think this ought to pay for one of those floral horseshoes they used to hang around necks at the track. Will you see that he gets one in the name of the bar?"

"Sure," he said. "Speed would like that."

I pushed out another fifty. "Put this one away so that all the regulars can drink on Speed until it's gone. I was going to give this to him today, and if he could voice his opinion, I'm sure he'd say to let the boys drink it up."

For the first time I saw some emotion in his face. "You're right, mister. Speed would think that was going out in style. And the guys in here will like the idea. Who will I tell them it's from?"

"Don't," I said. "The horseshoe wreath is from a guy who likes winners and the drinks are from Speed. That's all." I added ten dollars to the money, putting it in the trough. "Have a drink yourself." I turned and walked out and down to the Cadillac. I pulled away and headed back toward the Beach.

I stopped in a restaurant and bar where no one would think of looking for me. I had a drink at the bar, then went to the phone booth and made a call to Lieutenant Dillman.

"Milo March," I said when he answered. "Do you know who Speed Harris was?"

"The jockey?"

"The same."

"What do you mean was?" he asked. "The last I heard he was turned on wine somewhere in Miami. What about him?"

"He was turned on wine but he's graduated. He's now a resident in the Miami Morgue. Someone shot him not long ago. On the street near the mission where he lived—if you can call it that. Several people saw it happen, but

I think you'll find that no one got a description of the two men in the car or of the car or the license number. But you might find out what they do have and what kind of gun killed him."

"Why?"

"I think that it's part of our case."

"What would he have to do with that?"

"He was trying to get information for me, and I think he may have asked too many questions. He wanted and needed the money. You might find out what bookie joint he went to when he had money and who else made a habit of going there. Then sit on the information until you hear from me again."

"Wait a minute," he said. "Where are you now?"

"Out, trying to forget what happened," I said and hung up.

I went back to the bar and ordered another drink. I sipped drinks slowly until it was dark. Then I got in the car and drove up to the dock where Aristotle Murphy's boat was tied up. I parked the car in front of his boat, walked up to it and called out to him.

"Come aboard," he shouted from below.

By the time I stepped onto the boat, he was there. "Thought it sounded like you," he said. "Come below."

I followed him down the steps. It looked pretty much as it had before. The radio was playing soft music. There was a chess set on the table and it looked as if he'd been playing against himself.

"I'm glad to see you, lad," he said. "Will you join me in a glass of grog?"

"Not just yet, if you'll forgive me," I said. "I want you

to take me on a very short ride, and when we return I'll have a drink with you."

"Aye," he said. He finished his drink and put the chess set away. He went up to the deck and was soon back down. I could tell by the feel of the boat that he had cast off. He started the motor and began backing away from the dock.

"It's to the rear of the house of the barbarian?" he asked.

"It is."

"It's not far," he said. "Perhaps it's better if we do it without the running lights. How close in do you want to get?"

"As near as you can without tipping our hand."

"Aye." He'd already backed away from the dock and was beginning to move forward. He revved up the motor for a few minutes, then suddenly cut it.

"It is best," he said quietly, "if we coast in from here so that they won't hear the motors. Don't worry about it. I know this old girl like the back of me hand."

"Who's worrying?" I asked. I wanted to light a cigarette but decided it wasn't a good idea. The only sound was the slap of the water against the side of the boat.

Then suddenly there was another sound. There was music floating out over the water, and I realized we were right behind Bacci's house. Less than a hundred yards.

There were lights in the house and the faint sound of voices just under the music. The backyard was huge and surrounded by an iron fence. I could see the gate was padlocked, but that would be no problem. There was something else that would. I suddenly spotted two black shapes prowling over the lawn, their noses pointed in our direction. Dobermans. They didn't bark but just walked and looked at us.

"I've seen enough," I said. "Let's go."

He kicked on the motor and the boat surged ahead. Just as we started, a back door in the house opened and light streamed out to cover the two dogs.

Then something new was added. There was the sharp crack of a gun and a bullet hit the water near the boat and skidded across the top of the water. It reminded me of the flat rocks we used to throw on the water when I was a kid. But there was a difference.

8

Aristotle now had the boat at full throttle, and suddenly he threw it around to the left. At the same time, I heard another shot, but it obviously missed us. There didn't seem to be anything ahead of us, and Aristotle cut off his running lights.

A few minutes later we were back and secured in the berth. Aristotle cut the motor and leaned back, laughing. "That was a bit of fun, eh, lad?" he said. "Now, why do you suppose the lord of the manor was so touchy?"

"I guess he likes his privacy."

"How come you didn't shoot back?" he asked.

"This was just a friendly visit. You don't shoot people you don't even know."

"Oh, yes, the British tradition. First, you have to be introduced. I suppose you saw the dogs?"

"Sure. Nice-looking animals. I must try to find a friendly veterinarian."

"Why?"

"To get tranquilizers that are strong enough to give both of them a restful nap."

"Oh, yes. How about that glass of grog now, Milo?"

"I thought you'd never ask."

He got two glasses and poured generously from the bottle of rum. He pushed one across to me.

"Thanks," I said. "Do you have another glass?"

He looked puzzled but he reached for another glass and put it in front of me. I took the glass and turned it upside down. " 'And in your blissful errand reach the spot where once I sat,' " I quoted, " 'turn down an empty glass.' "

"Oh, yes," he said in delight, "I should have recognized it. Who died?"

"A little man who once was a big man. He died this afternoon. Rather violently. Because of me."

"They did it?" he asked, pointing in the direction of Bacci's house.

"Yes."

"Who was he?"

"He was known as Speed Harris. In better days he was a man who had a way with horses. You may have heard of him."

"Ah, yes, the jockey. I knew his name when I was a member of the Establishment and fell into their bad habits."

"What did you do in the Establishment?"

"I was a shaper of minds. I was what is called a professor, although I'm not sure what it meant. In the meantime, let's drink to your absent friend."

We drank. "Why did they kill him?" he asked.

"Because he was trying to get information for me. I guess that too much wine made him get careless."

He was silent while he took another long pull at the

rum. "I do happen to know a veterinarian. A good friend at the bottle and a fine chess player. When do you need the tranquilizer?"

"Tomorrow or the next day. I'm not sure."

"I'll have it for you."

"I'll drink to that," I said. "Do you have a marine phone?"

"Yes."

"I'll want to go back there tomorrow night or the night after that. I'll let you know."

"I'll be here."

"Okay," I said with a grin. "I'll tell you the rest of it when I come back." I finished my drink and took fifty dollars from my pocket. I put it on the table. "This is for services over and beyond the call of duty. I still owe you fifty, maybe more. Just say that it's from the insurance company . . . or from Speed Harris. Spend it all on grog, or a broad, or any silly thing you can think of. But just don't bug me about it. I make Establishment money, I do anti-Establishment things and I couldn't care less either way. I dig Marlowe and Villon. If I had lived in their period I would have been like them, and if they lived now they would be like me. Do you understand me?"

"Yes," he said. "That is why I help you. Not for any other reason. Don't you understand that?"

"I'm tired of guessing. I have only one philosophy. Survival. I'll explain it so there are no problems about the rest of our agreement. This afternoon I killed a man. I had only one reaction. I felt extreme pleasure because I had lived and he had not. I might point out to you that this is fairly normal in any period. The businessman today who saves his business and destroys a competitor feels the same thing. So does the soldier who is successful in his business. At the same time, I weep for Speed Harris who couldn't survive. Does that make sense to you?"

"Completely, lad," he said. "Will you have another drink?"

"Not now. I promised you that we will spend an evening together and we will. But first I have a couple of unpleasant things to do, and I can't relax until they are behind me. Many people complain that I drink a lot. I do, but I also do the things that have to be done. I'll either see you tomorrow or talk to you. And you will get the tranquilizers for me?"

"That I will, lad. I presume that you want to put them in some lovely meat?"

"That's the general idea. Thanks, Aristotle."

I got up and left. The Cadillac was still out front. I climbed in and drove back to the hotel. I didn't even look to see if the other car was out front. I turned my car over to the boy and went inside. I stopped at the desk to ask if I'd had any calls or messages. There were none. I went on into the bar.

Buck was still there but he wasn't working. He was on the other side of the bar. I sat down next to him and told the bartender to bring us two drinks. When he brought them I asked him for an empty glass. He brought it and I turned it upside down on the bar.

"Did you hear the news?" I asked Buck.

He shook his head. "Nothing but the usual. Which broad just met a wonderful guy, which guy just met a wonderful broad and who had just scammed someone out of money."

116

"We're drinking," I said, "to an absent friend." I lifted my glass and he did the same. We drank. "Speed Harris was killed this afternoon. Because he was trying to get information for me."

He looked shocked. "Who killed him?"

"A little man with a gun and a little man, who thinks he's big, who gives the orders."

"How?"

"Shot. From a car that was passing through the street where the mission is in Miami. And continued to pass through."

"My God," he said. He motioned for the bartender to give us two more drinks. "I liked Speed."

"So did I, even though I met him only once. The second meeting was supposed to be today."

"But why?"

"I'll never know," I said. "He called me here at the hotel. I guess he thought he had some information for me. And I guess somebody else thought he did, too."

"Where did it happen?"

"In front of a bar just up the street from the mission."

"Know anything about the funeral?"

"I was told that the mission would probably take care of that. I paid for a floral horseshoe like they give winners and set up some future drinks for his friends in the bar next to the mission. I thought he might like that."

"Yeah," he said. "He would. I guess he didn't have much to live for, but it's still lousy to hear about him going that way."

I nodded and finished my drink. I was about to go phone the girl upstairs when I was paged for a phone call. I went over and picked up the house phone. I identified myself and the call was put through.

"Milo?" she asked. It was a nice voice, and my name was pronounced with the careful inflection that airline stewardesses often use.

"Hello, Annette," I said. "When did you get back in town?"

"About an hour ago. Did you miss me?"

"Naturally. I thought maybe you'd forgotten to call."

"How could I forget? I spent all my life thinking a girl was safe on a balcony. Look, Milo, I have to do laundry and things like that tonight. But I might be free tomorrow night—if you're interested."

"I'm interested," I said. "I will be working, I think, during the early part of the evening. But it shouldn't take too long. I'll call you, or if you'd rather, you can come over here and wait for me. I shouldn't be out for more than a couple of hours. Then we can have dinner . : . on the balcony."

"That sounds great. Did you miss me?"

"Terribly," I said gravely. "Things have been very dull here."

She laughed to prove that she didn't believe me. "I'll see you tomorrow night."

When she hung up, I used the house phone to call Betty Carlson's room.

"Milo," I said when she answered. "I just got back to the hotel. Want to meet me downstairs?"

"I'll be right down," she said. "At the bar?"

"Where else?"

I went back to the bar and ordered another drink.

Buck was still sitting there and I bought him another drink. "I'll have this one," he said, "but then I have to take a hike. The old lady will think I'm chasing some chippy."

"Don't worry about it, Buck. I'll tell her it's not true."

"If you told her, she'd be sure it was true."

"Just because you're on this side of the bar," I told him, "you don't have to start sounding like all the customers."

Betty showed up and took the stool next to me. "Hi," she said. "Hello, Buck."

"Hello, Miss Carlson," he said.

"Were you two talking about something interesting?" she asked.

"Sure," I said. I motioned for the bartender to give her a martini. "We were talking about broads. What else is interesting?"

"Oh, men!"

"Come to think of it, I guess you're right," I said. "I am pretty interesting now that you mention it."

"You do make a lovely couple all by yourself," she said sweetly.

"Wait a minute. I'm supposed to get the good lines around here."

"I think he's jealous," Buck said. "And I'm going home before my old lady gets jealous."

He said good night and left. We had two more martinis and then went upstairs. I called room service and ordered two dinners and a pitcher of martinis. We had dinner out on the balcony. It was a beautiful night with the moonlight stalking the waves.

Later we went to bed. But it was different than the other night. It had been a long hard day and I went to sleep with her in my arms.

Maybe I was getting old, I thought, when I awakened a couple of hours later. I looked at her. Her eyelids were beginning to tremble. She had the warm sweet smell of a woman just emerging from sleep, and I discovered I wasn't getting old.

It was a good feeling. After we had experienced my rebirth, she was curled up against me, her head on my shoulder. I was thinking what I had to do. I hated to do it but the only alternative was worse for her.

"Jane," I said softly.

Her body tightened like a tightly stretched wire, then exploded as she tried to throw herself out of the bed. I held her close to me.

"Take it easy, honey," I said softly. "I'm not your enemy. I'm not out to kill you or arrest you. I'm probably the only friend you have, and your only chance of coming through this is by listening to me. I can, and will, help you all I can."

She stayed where she was, but her entire body was trembling and her breath was no more than a rattle in her throat. "You knew all the time," she said. "None of it was real."

"That's not true," I told her. "I didn't know until after we made love the first time. I only knew then because of the scar. But that didn't make any difference the other times."

She shuddered. "How do I know that's true?" Her voice sounded like that of a little girl.

"You're bright enough to know it. When Wilma Leeds

120

was killed, you knew they'd be looking for you, too. That's when you changed your hair, your looks and your name again. And your hotel. Why do you think they killed Wilma and wanted to kill you?"

"Why?"

"Because the two of you were the only ones who could testify against them in court. By 'them' I mean Jack Daly and Bobby Dixon. In the first place, I'll bet you that they shortchanged both of you. How much did they give you?"

"Five thousand dollars," she said weakly. "They said there would be more."

"Sure. And Wilma collected what they expected to give you. Nice boys."

"Wilma," she said, "was in love with Jack Daly and would do anything he wanted her to. The idea was that I was supposed to be Bobby Dixon's girl friend, but I couldn't stand him. I wouldn't even stay in the same hotel with Wilma."

"Why did you fall for it, honey?"

"I guess," she said vaguely, "I thought that Jack was something special, too. And it seemed like a lovely dream."

"They always do. Want a drink, honey?"

"Please."

I got out of bed and poured two drinks. There wasn't any ice, but I figured she wouldn't miss it at the time. I handed one glass to her.

"What happens now?" she asked in a dull voice. "Are you going to arrest me or something?"

"No, Jane. I have no authority to arrest anyone. I'm not even going to call the cops on you. And I'm certainly not going to turn you over to Jack Daly. If you'll listen to me, I can help you, but that's all."

"How can you help me?"

"Look at the situation, Jane. You and Wilma did take the bonds and securities at the suggestion of Jack Daly. Daly and Dixon had no idea of really sharing with you or of letting you live to testify against them. You did manage to escape that part of it up until now—but Wilma didn't. And you were left hiding in a hole, never knowing when they might find you. They are not just playboys. In addition to killing Wilma, they have tried to kill me twice and will try again. There is another side to them. What do you think they've done with the securities you and Wilma took and turned over to them?"

"They . . . they said," she faltered, "that they could get rid of them through banks."

"No chance, honey. The loss of the securities was discovered too quickly, otherwise they could have borrowed money from banks by using the securities as collateral. But they had an easier way of turning them into cash. Did you ever read in your newspaper about organized crime, known by such various names as the Syndicate, the Mafia or the Cosa Nostra?"

"Yes . . . I've heard of them. But surely Jack Daly was not part of anything like that."

"Part of it, no. But Jack Daly did sell the securities to a member of organized crime here in Florida. I don't know how much he got, but it might have been as high as four or five hundred thousand dollars and not less than three hundred thousand. He gave each of you five thousand dollars, taking back whatever Wilma had left when he killed her. The man who bought the securities from

Daly then sold them to another hood in Chicago and made some profit for himself. That man, in turn, sold them to another man in another city and got his profit. The idea was that they would eventually end up somewhere in Europe where they couldn't be traced anywhere."

She was silent for a minute, gnawing on her lip. I poured two drinks and put one in front of her.

"Is that really what they planned?" she asked finally.

"It's what they planned. It's also what they've done up to this point. You've had some luck. Their idea was larceny, laying and leaving—both of you for dead."

"What do you want me to do, Milo?"

"Save yourself," I said simply. "There are two things facing you. First, there are a number of men right here in Miami Beach who want to kill you. A few of them are professional killers. You have escaped so far by sheer luck. You found a rabbit burrow and stayed in it. You were even lucky that we didn't go out that first time we had dinner, because they've been following me. After I knew who you were, I made sure that we didn't leave the hotel together."

"If . . . if they're as bad as you say, how can I ever get away from them? I can't stay in this hotel the rest of my life."

"That's true, honey. The Miami Beach police would pick you up if they knew where you were. But they'd only hold you until the New York City authorities extradited you. I'm not certain you'd be safe in jail here."

"You mean there's nothing for me to do?" She was starting to shake again.

"No. I don't mean that. There's a chain of events.

123

First, you and Wilma took the bonds and securities. You turned them over to Jack Daly and Bobby Dixon. They turned them over to someone else and received money. From there they have passed on to at least two other persons. Wilma is dead. You are the only person who can say who got them from you. Jack Daly and Bobby Dixon are the only ones who can tell who they sold them to."

"I don't understand."

"I think," I said slowly, "that all of the men here in Florida will be arrested—or dead—within the next twenty-four or forty-eight hours. That doesn't mean, however, that they will be convicted or even go to trial. You are the only person who can send Daly and Dixon to prison. They are the only persons who can send the others to prison, and they will only do it if they are convinced that it will help them to some degree."

"I still don't understand what you're saying, Milo. If they are guilty, won't they go to prison?"

"Not necessarily—especially when they have plenty of money. And they do."

"But I *will* go to prison, won't I? Or, if I don't, I'll be killed. Isn't that what you're trying to say?"

"Not exactly, honey. If I'm right, and I'll know tomorrow, the bonds and securities will be recovered. That will make everyone on the other side a little happier. If you give yourself up in New York and agree to testify against Daly and Dixon, the authorities will take that into consideration. Your testimony should be enough to convict them. And, under the circumstances, I'm pretty sure that you will get off with probation. You will be able to work, and when the probation is up, you can vanish from official view. Isn't that better than running the rest of your life from both guns and the law?"

"I guess so. But if I do testify against them, it'll still be just my word against theirs, won't it?"

"Not completely. Where did you and Wilma meet them?"

"At a night club over in New Jersey. We had gone there with a girl Wilma had worked with before she came to the place where I worked."

"Do you remember the name of the club and the name of the girl you went with?"

"Yes."

"What about Daly and Dixon? Did they use those names when you met them?"

"Yes."

"How many times," I asked, "did you see them in the New York area after that first meeting?"

"I'm not sure. Eight or nine times."

"Do you remember where?"

"I think I remember the places."

"Did they tell you where they were staying and did you ever call them there?"

"I didn't but Wilma did, and I was with her some of the times when she called."

"Were they using their real names there?"

"Yes."

"What happened about the bonds and securities?"

"Well," she said, "they knew where we worked and what we did and one night, when we'd all had a lot to drink, they suggested that we get all the securities we could. At the time, it seemed more like a joke than anything else. The next morning before we went to work,

Jack Daly called Wilma at home and reminded her what we were to do. We were to take the bonds and securities shortly before the end of the day. Then he gave her the name and address of a beauty parlor on Long Island and said he'd make appointments for us for that evening under the names of Loraine Wilks and Betty Keith. We were to go right from the office, but not together."

"Remember the name of the beauty parlor and maybe the girl who worked on you?"

"Yes. It was . . ."

"You don't have to tell me," I interrupted. "Just tell the police. They'll be able to check all of those things out to support your story. How did you get the securities out of the office?"

"We both had large handbags and we divided the securities up between us."

"All right. Then what happened?"

"Well, we went to the beauty shop and had our appearances changed. From there, we went to our separate apartments, packed clothes and went to the airport. Jack had already made reservations for us under the new names. Oh, yes, I forgot. . . . He'd told us to go to our banks on our lunch hour and draw out enough money for the plane tickets to Miami. We left New York that night. Jack and Bobby met us at the Miami airport. They took the bonds and dropped us at the hotel where they had made reservations for us."

"How did you feel about all this while it was going on?" I asked.

"I was scared," she said. "I think Wilma was, too. But at the same time there was a kind of excitement. I can't explain it. . . ."

126

"You don't have to. I understand it. What happened next?"

"Jack gave us some money. Wilma was seeing him every night. I didn't like Bobby so I stayed home. Then we decided it would be smarter if I moved to another hotel. I did and just stayed there until the morning I heard on television that Wilma had been killed. Oh, they didn't give her real name but they did show a photograph of the body and I recognized it. I could only think of one thing to do. I changed my hair and makeup again and moved here under another name. I was afraid to say hello to anyone until I met you."

I reached out and stroked her hair. "Believe me, honey, we're both better off because of it." I made two more drinks for us and lit two cigarettes. "It'll be bad but not as bad as you expect."

"What am I going to do, Milo?" she asked.

"I can't tell you what to do," I said, "but this is what I suggest. Stay here with me tonight. Sometime in the morning I should hear from New York. And they should have the bonds back. And then I will arrange for you to fly back to New York and surrender to a friend of mine who's a lieutenant there. He will see that you're protected in every way. He's fuzz, but he's also a nice guy."

"When do I have to go back?" she asked.

"You don't have to do anything," I said, "but if you're smart, you'll take the first plane you can get tomorrow after I talk to him."

"By myself?"

"Yes."

"Can't you go with me?" she asked.

"Didn't you hear anything I said? We don't dare leave

this hotel together. If we do, the wrong people will suddenly get very interested. And I will be very busy for a day or two longer. And it won't be very safe. Don't you want to live?"

"Yes, Milo."

"Then listen to me. I'm trying to save your life. I know my business and you don't know yours—at least the one you're involved in at the moment."

"Yes, Milo."

She sounded too meek. I quickly poured two more drinks, making one of them stronger than the other one. I gave that one to her.

"I'll be back in a couple of days," I said, "and then I'll see you. In the meantime, you sleep here tonight and you'll be safe. Then we'll make the rest of the plans."

"Whatever you say, Milo."

I thought it was getting a little out of hand. As soon as she had finished her drink, I poured another one for her. Finally, she curled up in the bed and went to sleep without finishing the other drink. I made sure that the door was locked and placed a chair in front of it just in the event that somebody picked the lock. Then I got my .38 from the closet and put it next to my side of the bed. Then I turned out the light and went to sleep with my arms around her.

She was still asleep when I awakened the next morning. I listened to her breathing for a minute, then went in and had a fast shower and shave. I dressed and then checked her again. She was still sleeping heavily, but it was late enough. I shook her awake.

"Go in and take your shower, honey," I said. "I'll

order some breakfast for us. You stay in there until I tell you that it's time to come out. You want a drink with breakfast?"

"I think I'd better," she said and it sounded as if she was right. She got up and went to the bathroom. "Anything you suggest." She didn't walk too steadily but she still made a pretty picture.

I called room service and ordered two breakfasts of scrambled eggs and bacon, plus toast and a pot of coffee. For good measure, I ordered a double Bloody Mary for her and a double martini for me.

The waiter arrived with the order. He wheeled in the table and removed the one from the night before. I knocked on the bathroom door and she came out. She still hadn't dressed, but the shower had put color in her skin. She looked great and I told her so.

"Thank you," she said with an embarrassed laugh. "I'm afraid I'm really not used to this."

"To what?"

"Well, spending the night in someone's room and then walking around without my clothes on."

"It'll grow on you, honey," I said. I handed her the Bloody Mary. "There's only one way to greet every morning."

"What do you mean?"

"Just think of it as the first day of the rest of your life."

"I'm afraid that isn't much to look forward to."

"Nonsense. It'll be a little rough at first, but there's no need to wear it around your neck the rest of your life. And you can always remember that it's a better life than Wilma Leeds will have."

She shuddered. "I'll try to. And thanks, Milo, for holding me all night. It helped."

"It was my pleasure," I said. "Now, let's eat breakfast before it gets cold. We slept a little late this morning, and so we should get some news from New York before too long."

We didn't say anything until we reached the coffee. "I guess a good breakfast does help," she said then with a smile. "What do we do now?"

"Wait to hear from my friend in New York. If he doesn't call soon, I'll call him. Then we make a reservation for you on a plane to New York. On second thought, it might be better if we made the reservation first. That way, we can tell him what plane you'll be on and he'll be there to meet you."

"Can't you go with me?" she asked wistfully.

"I can't, honey. I still have work to do here. I can't even go to the airport with you. It would be too dangerous."

"Will . . . will he put me in jail when I get there?"

"I honestly don't know. He will put you in protective custody. Then you'll have to stay in either a special cell or a hotel room where you can be guarded while there's danger to you."

"All right," she said.

I picked up the phone and called the airlines. I got her put on the twelve o'clock flight under the name of Betty Carlson. I hung up and looked at her. "You'll be all right, Jane. When you leave the hotel, I doubt if they'll recognize you. I'll be somewhere, however, so that if anyone does try to follow you, I'll be around so that nothing happens."

"Well, I'd better go pack my things."

"Wait until I talk to New York. I want you to hear the conversation." I picked up what was left of my double martini and finished it. I had just put the glass down when the phone rang. I lifted the receiver and said hello.

"Milo," he said, "Johnny Rockland. I guess I owe you one."

"You got the bonds and the securities?"

"All of them. Or, at least, the Boston police have them. And the messenger and the man they were delivered to. He's a guy known as Bicksy Gordon. Ever hear of him?"

"Gordon? Sure. He's a big man in Boston. Who was the messenger? Granetti?"

"That's the one. I'm not sure that the case against him can be made to stick. The Boston cops wanted to be sure that they got the man who was accepting the delivery. They did, a few seconds after he had the bag in his chubby little hands. It may be tough to prove that it's the same bag that Granetti carried from the plane, but there's a clear case of possession against Gordon. How's it going on your end?"

"I think," I said, "that it will be pretty much cleared up in the next day or two. At least, as well as it can be cleared without someone copping out. There may be enough pressure on the two men, Daly and Dixon, to make them implicate Bacci, the big fish. That is, of course, if they're all still alive."

"Sounds like you've got a job ahead of you. Getting any help down there?"

"Yeah. A local cop named Lieutenant Wayne Dillman. He's giving as much help as I'll accept—which is less than he wants to give. Remember his name. You may have to work out a deal with him."

"What kind of a deal?" Johnny asked.

"Dillman has been working on the murder case down here. He wants Daly and Dixon for that. Daly for committing the murder, Dixon probably as an accessory. Bacci furnished an alibi for them. I'm not sure that the murder rap can be made to stick, but it might. Make a deal with Dillman to turn them over to you. I feel sure you can get a conviction on working out the theft, receiving stolen property and possibly the sale of it."

"The deal sounds possible but the second part of it may not be as easy as that. Remember that your Daly and Dixon can only be convicted through the two girls who did the stealing. One of them is dead and the other one may be. At least, nobody has found her."

"Wrong."

"What do you mean?" He sounded excited.

"There's a girl taking a twelve o'clock plane from Miami today. Meet her up there at the airport. Her name is Betty Carlson. You won't recognize her, but when she gets off the plane she will go to the Eastern Airlines desk and ask for plain John Rockland." I looked at her and she nodded. "Be good to her, Johnny, and take extra special care of her. She's your witness, and without her you have no case against the important ones."

"I'll wrap her up in cotton and see that nothing even bumps her," he said fervently.

"That includes," I said, "taking good care of her after it's over."

"I will, Milo. The best she can expect, however, is probation. But I don't think there will be any problem about that. Once we get a conviction on those two, we can let Florida try their luck at the murder rap. Milo, I take back all the things I've said about you in the past."

"I'll keep in touch with you, Johnny." I hung up. I went over and sat next to her and took her hand.

"It's all set, honey," I said. "He'll meet you at the airport and see that you're safe. And he says that the worst that can happen to you is probation."

"You're sure it's going to be all right?"

"Positive," I said. "Now you run along and get packed. I'll meet you down in the lobby. You can get checked out, and we'll have a drink in the bar together before you leave. And if you need any money, I'll give it to you."

"Oh, no, I have plenty of money. I spent very little of the money Jack Daly gave me. I'll be right down." She stood up.

"One small suggestion. I think if you were to put your clothes on first it might create less of a disturbance."

A startled look came over her face. "Oh! I was so comfortable I guess I forgot. I'm sorry, Milo."

"You don't have to be. Personally, I like you the way you are. I imagine that most of the other male guests would feel the same—but it might cause a riot. I'll see you in the bar." I kissed her lightly on the cheek and left.

Downstairs, I went to the front of the lobby and looked out the door. The faithful car was back on duty. There were two men in it. The one behind the wheel was Ketcher. The other was Hackett.

On the way back, I stopped at the desk and got my thousand dollars from the safe. Then I went on into the bar. Buck came over and I ordered a drink.

"Working again, I see," he said when he brought it.

133

"Certainly," I said. "What you don't seem to understand, my dear Buck, is that most of my efforts are devoted to brain work."

"That's why you carry a gun?"

"That is only in case the brain breaks down. Now, run along and polish a glass. I am being joined pretty soon by a young lady, and the brain work must be done before then."

He muttered something under his breath and departed. I sat back and thought about the situation. There was just one flaw in the plan. I was certainly right about thinking that if the girl and I left together, they would follow. I felt pretty sure that they wouldn't follow her if she went by taxi. The flaw was that they just might recognize her. There was no way I could be positive about that. Without her, the whole case would blow up.

My first thought was to call Lieutenant Dillman and have him pick up the two hoods long enough for her taxi to get away. But even that might not work. They might get the number of the cab and work the driver over until he told them where he had taken her. I felt I had to make certain that they were out of it.

A few minutes later I had the only idea that made any sense—at least to me. I told Buck to make another drink and went back to the front of the lobby. A bellboy brought one of the boys who parked the cars in to see me. I gave him ten dollars to bring the Cadillac out of the garage and park it across the street a few feet behind the waiting car and to leave my keys in it.

With what I had in mind, I thought I'd better play safe. I went upstairs to my room and once more taped the small holster to my left leg and put the .25 in it. I returned to the bar.

"Get all your heavy thinking done?" Buck asked sarcastically.

"All done," I said cheerfully. "I always like to get it over with early, and then I don't have to worry about it if any problems come up. Which reminds me I have to make a phone call." I went over to the phone and called Lieutenant Dillman.

"Milo March," I said when he answered.

"It was nice of you to phone," he said. Everyone was being sarcastic with me. "I trust you're enjoying your stay in Florida."

"I got no complaints. The women are beautiful and willing and the cops are polite."

"I suppose you called to ask a favor?"

"You wrong me, Lieutenant. I've been thinking that I might have some important information for you tonight, and it suddenly occurred to me that I don't have your home phone number."

He groaned. "We don't get overtime, you know."

"Sorry," I said. "If you'd rather that I just phoned the station and gave it to anyone who answered the phone, I'll do that. I wouldn't want to disturb you."

"I'm sure you wouldn't. Why don't you ask for simple things, like having a ticket fixed? Don't answer that. I know you'd tell me it was illegal. All right." He gave me the number and hung up. I went back to the bar.

"Calling a broad, I suppose?" Buck asked.

"Not me, Buck. They call me. It's easier that way. No, I was speaking with one of Miami Beach's law enforcement officers. A splendid bunch of men."

"Now I know you're sick. I've heard the things you say about cops, and usually I had to cover my ears. All this can mean is that you just conned some poor unsuspecting cop. How's the case coming?"

"Thanks to my hard work, I think it'll be more or less wound up today or tomorrow. In a way, it's too bad. I'll miss your splendid drinks."

"What did you do—get lucky? I can swear you haven't done any work."

"Buck," I said in a hurt tone of voice, "you don't understand the finer things in life. When I first got into this racket, I decided that I didn't want to pound pavements or lurk around dark alleys. There seemed to be only one solution. In my business, unlike that of official cops, there is one advantage. There is always the problem that some-one is dipping into the till. There's usually no more than three or four, sometimes no more than two, possible suspects. So I just push them around a little and the guilty finally start pushing back a little. Then I know I'm on the home trail. Besides, I'm getting too old to chase miscreants down the street. It's easier to let them chase me down the street."

"For this they pay you? You have to be the biggest thief in the country."

"Thank you, Buck. It's the nicest compliment you ever paid me. But you do forget one thing—it creates more hospital bills."

"Which go on your expense account," he growled. The phone behind the bar rang and he went over to answer it. He said a few words and came back. "Well, you were right about one thing."

"I'm always right," I said calmly. "What is it this time?"

"About the broads calling you. That was Miss Carlson. She said to tell you that she'd be right down."

"She has excellent taste in men." I glanced at my watch. "She has plenty of time, so we must give her an excellent send-off."

"What do you mean?"

"She's checking out shortly."

"Why?"

"How do I know? I guess she has to go back to her school job or whatever it is. Whatever, it's her business and not mine."

"Yeah, I guess you're right," Buck said. "I wasn't really trying to stick my nose into her business, but I was curious."

"I know," I said gently. "I didn't say you shouldn't be curious. Some day, maybe I'll be able to tell you why she's checking out. But in the meantime, the only thing that concerns us is that she should leave as happily as possible."

"I'll drink to that," he said. He looked as if he were going to say more but just then she came in and perched on the stool next to me.

"Here I am, Milo," she said. "How much time do I have?"

"Enough," I said. "I'll let you know. Buck, give the little lady whatever she wants. Make it special."

"Certainly. What would you like, Miss Carlson?"

"I don't know. Maybe a whiskey sour."

"Coming right up." He made the whiskey sour and a drink for me and came back. He looked at me uncer-

137

tainly. "These are on the house. Both of you keep me company during the lonesome hours."

"Thank you, Buck. You have been nice to me since I've been here."

"What do you mean *have* been?" he asked indignantly. "I intend to go on being nice to you. You're a real lady."

I looked at her and saw her eyes were misting up. I looked away before she could realize that I had noticed.

"Of course, you would, Buck," she said. "I merely used that expression because I'm leaving in a few minutes."

"You are?" His tone of surprise wasn't very good but I'm sure it fooled her. "How come? Your vacation up?"

"Yes, my vacation is up." I could hear the sadness in her voice. "Maybe I'll be able to come back some day."

"I sure hope so, Miss Carlson. We'll miss you, won't we, Milo?"

"Yes," I said. "You more than me. I will see her as soon as I go back in a couple of days."

"You will, Milo?" she asked.

"Sure, honey. I know how to get in touch with you. Now, to a good flight."

We drank and then had a couple more, and it was time for her to leave.

She had already checked out, so I got a bellboy to carry the bags out and have the doorman whistle a cab from around the corner. We waited at the door with me standing behind her so there was less chance of Ketcher and Hackett seeing me. The cab drove up. I kissed her and still tried to be masked by her. As she got into the cab, I turned to the right and walked past the cab, then hurriedly went down the exit driveway. I risked one

138

glance at the car across the street and saw that both men seemed to be looking at the taxi.

I scurried across the street and got into the Cadillac by the time the taxi drove down the ramp. It turned to the left and passed the car ahead of me. I already had the motor started.

I had been right about not overlooking anything. They pulled out in pursuit of the cab. I followed them. I waited for three blocks, then swerved to the left and passed them. As soon as I was past the front of their car, I turned in front of them and slammed on the brakes. There was a squeal of tires as they tried to avoid hitting me. By that time I had the Cadillac in park and was jumping out. I rushed back to their car and by the time I reached the front window I had my gun out.

"Hello, boys," I said. "How's everything at the Bacci Rancho?"

9

They had been so busy avoiding an accident they didn't have a good look at me until then. Carl Ketcher, who was behind the wheel, reached for his gun as soon as he recognized me. Then he stopped as he saw my gun.

"That's a good boy," I said sweetly. "Keep it up and I might let you stay alive a little longer."

"What the hell do you want, March?" he asked.

"You've been following me for some time," I said, "so I thought I'd follow you once and give you a bit of advice—in memory of the late Meyer Devlin."

"We're busy," Ketcher said.

"Not too busy for an old friend, I hope? And not nearly as busy as you will be unless you do exactly as I say."

He made a rude suggestion. I reached through the window and hit him across the nose with the barrel of the gun. "How does that grab you for openers? Go ahead and be my guests. Why don't you do a countdown and then both draw at once? As far as I'm concerned, it's open season on you."

Both of them were breathing hard. Ketcher reached

up slowly with one hand and wiped the blood from his face. "We're going to get you, March. You've been lucky so far, but, so help me, we'll get you if it's the last thing we do."

"It will be," I said sweetly. "Okay. I'm busy, too. Back up your car, make a U-turn and head back the other way as fast as you can. Why don't you drive up and pay a visit to Antonio? He probably misses Hackett there. He might even fix up your nose for you, Ketcher."

He started to make another rude suggestion, but I interrupted him. "Start moving. . . . Or do you want another facial?"

He started the car and began to back up. I stepped back so that my car shielded me if he decided to catch me with the fender. I still had the gun on them, but I held it close so that it would be difficult for anyone to see it from the street.

Traffic wasn't too heavy on Collins, so he soon found an opening and swung around with screeching tires.

I got back in the Cadillac and drove slowly ahead, keeping a watch in the rear-view mirror. As I expected, they drove a little more than two blocks and then made another fast U-turn to bring them behind me. But they overlooked one thing. Just as they were half way through the turn, a squad car appeared coming toward us. As soon as they saw the other car, the cops opened their siren. I watched with interest as Ketcher hesitated, then finally pulled to the curb.

I stepped on the accelerator, laughing to myself. It would have been all right if they had come on after me, but this was a slight extra break. They were both so angry that they would probably start arguing with the cops instead of trying money, which was the universal language in Miami Beach. Their tête-à-tête with the cops would provide enough extra time. And I did want to save the real showdown with them. I knew I now had them so angry that they were ripe.

Since I like to hedge my bets, I continued on to Miami, going as fast as I could and still keep within the speed limit. It wasn't long before I reached the airport. I parked and went inside. It didn't take me long to discover the gate where the passengers were waiting to board the flight to New York.

She was in the line, looking slightly forlorn. I stepped back to a spot where it would give me a good view of the terminal but one where she wouldn't be apt to see me. Then I concentrated on watching both approaches to the gate.

I heard the final call over the loudspeaker and risked a glance toward the gate. The passengers were already filing through. I waited until the gate was closed and all the passengers were on the plane. Then I walked over to where I could see the field. The plane glided down the runway and lifted gracefully into the air. I waited another five minutes just to make sure that something didn't immediately develop that would make the plane return to the airport.

I went back to the car. Just as I was driving out of the parking lot, I saw a car driving in. In it were Ketcher and Hackett. They seemed to be in a hurry. I smiled to myself and kept on going. At first I had thought I wouldn't go back to the hotel until night, but I changed my mind.

I stopped on the way and bought a large package of hamburger in a supermarket. Then I went on to the hotel and turned the car over to the parking boy. I left the hamburger in the back seat of the car. I went inside and checked at the desk. There was a message to call Lieutenant Dillman. I made the call.

"Well," he said when he came on the phone, "I did you another favor today."

"What was that?"

"You know those two boys who have been following you, Ketcher and Hackett?"

"I know them."

"I passed the word yesterday for all the cops to keep a watch for them and shake them up as much as possible. Today, a squad car caught them making a U-turn on Collins near your hotel. They were probably trying to get on your tail. Anyway, the officers not only gave them a ticket, but they found both of them carrying guns and made them come down here to have the gun permits and the registrations checked. By the time that was over, they must have lost you."

"Well, let's say it gave me a slight breathing spell."

"Where were you going?"

"Believe it or not, just to see a friend off at the airport. But they still might have made it uncomfortable. You see, I was the one responsible for them making that U-turn, and I suspect they may have been a little hot. They were just arriving at the airport as I left. They didn't see me leaving. But don't think I'm not grateful. I am."

"Sure," he said sourly. "But I still did you a favor. When are you going to do me one?"

143

"Maybe tonight. Don't go to bed too early. Is that all you wanted?"

"I just thought you might like to tell me what's going on with *our* case. After all, I might want to retire one of these days, and I'd hate to do it with a case hanging up in the air."

"I understand perfectly, sir. I will do my best, sir. Just make sure that the morgue is available in the event that I slip up somewhere." I hung up and went into the bar. Buck brought me a drink without being asked.

"She make the plane all right?" he asked.

"She made it all right."

"How's everything else going?"

"Everything else is going peachy." I emptied the drink and pushed the glass toward him. "Fill it up. I've got a long trip ahead of me."

"So that's how it's going," he said as he took the glass. He poured me a drink. "I was just trying to be neighborly."

"Everybody's neighborly," I reported, "but nobody's mowing the grass."

He went along with it. "Sorry to hear about that."

"Oh, it's all right. I wouldn't mind mowing the grass myself—but I don't smoke the stuff."

He laughed politely and moved away to polish another glass. I tossed off the second drink and decided it was time I made another phone call. I told Buck I'd see him later and went out to one of the public phones. I dialed the number and waited patiently. Finally, I was rewarded. Someone answered.

"Am I speaking to *the* Jack Daly?" I asked politely.

"I'm Jack Daly. Who are you?"

"Milo March."

"Go to hell," he said.

"I probably will, but I'm not in any hurry. I doubt if I will see you there. You're more apt to be floating around in limbo. I only called to see if you were having an open house any time this evening. Or do you have a date with another girl in the Everglades?"

"If I had an open house you wouldn't be welcome."

"I think I might," I said. "I have some information you might like to know."

"What?"

"I know where Jane Carlton is."

There was a moment of silence before he answered. "You mean you want to sell this information?"

"Not exactly. I might, however, be willing to trade it."

"For what?"

"I was thinking it's getting to the point where you should dump your friends Bobby and Angelo. It's time you stopped carrying all that excess weight. Anyway, he who dumps first lives longer. Or would you prefer a different trade?"

"What?" His voice was rasping.

"The information for your life. Think it over, Jack. I'll see you later." I put the receiver down gently. Then I went upstairs, stretched out on the bed and went to sleep.

Almost four hours had passed when I awakened. I felt rested and relaxed. I went in the bathroom and shaved and showered. I got dressed and used fresh tape to fasten the small holster to my left leg. I checked out both guns and then went downstairs. Buck had just gotten off work but was having a drink. I went over, sat beside him and ordered a drink from the new bartender.

"Where have you been?" Buck asked.

"Sleeping the sleep of the just and the pure. There's nothing like it. Now I'm ready for anything."

"Another big date?" he asked.

"If I'm right, it'll be a really big date. But not exactly the kind you think. If I'm lucky, I might have the other kind later."

"The airline stewardess?"

"Yeah."

"I thought it was about time for her to be back in town. Is that the reason you hustled Miss Carlson out of town?"

"Would I do a thing like that? Yes, I guess I would if the circumstances warranted it. But that wasn't what happened in this case. I was saving her from something worse than me."

"What could that be?"

I ordered another martini and another drink for Buck. "Maybe I'll tell you some time. But pretty soon I'm off to meet a friend of yours."

"Who?"

"Aristotle Murphy."

"Give my regards. What do you think of him?"

"I like him. He's a true eccentric, but I always like them."

"You mean a nut? Well, you're one yourself so you should like them."

"Buck, you always say the sweetest things. Now stop pouting because I won't tell you all my secrets, and I'll buy you another drink."

He laughed. "I'll go along with that. And I'll blame it

all on you when my wife complains of liquor on my breath."

"Just like all of you married men. The way to get around that is to kiss somebody else's wife."

"I'll tell her about that."

"A born fink." I motioned to the bartender and he brought two more drinks.

"Weren't you ever married?" Buck asked.

"Sure, I was married. It was a good many years ago, and it was fine while it lasted. The only trouble was my job. No woman wants a man who is seldom home. I never blamed her for that. She was right."

"Yeah, I can see that. Any children?"

"We adopted a Spanish boy I met on a job not long after we were married. I gave her custody of the boy. No good for him to have a father who's never at home either."

"How come you didn't think of getting into a new line of work?"

"I thought of it, but not for very long. I like my work. I like most of the places it takes me. It pays well with a lot of expense money thrown in. I meet a lot of beautiful broads. I also meet a lot of interesting people—and that includes a few bartenders."

"You drink too much," he said.

I laughed. "That's what a lot of people say. But did you ever see me under the influence?"

"No."

"If you broke it down by the number of hours I'm floating around each day, you'd find the total daily consumption is not so much. I like to drink, but not the way a lot of people do. They will go all day without a drink, or maybe just one cocktail at lunch, waiting until after five o'clock. Then they'll drink too fast to make up for the dry day and end up smashed before dinner."

"I guess you're right," he said. "I never thought of it that way, but I see a lot of it here. Vacationers will let go around noon, but the ones who are here on business wait until cocktail time, but, boy, do they go then."

"Your curiosity satisfied yet?"

"I guess so. My old lady is always telling me that I butt into people's business too much, but that comes from being a bartender. You listen to all the stuff that floats over the bar and start getting curious about the part you don't hear."

"I guess you're right. I've noticed that bartenders' ears bend in the direction of the most interesting conversation. Now, if you've satisfied your curiosity, it's dark and time for me to leave before I turn into a pumpkin. Is that all right with you?"

"Where are you going?"

"You see? You're prying again. I'll see you tomorrow, Buck."

"I suppose so," he said gloomily. "But, at least, you get in early before the interesting customers arrive."

"One more crack like that and I'll tell the bartender to take your last drink off my check," I said sternly. "Take it easy, Buck."

"Likewise, Milo. I'll mention you in my prayers tonight. I have a feeling you'll need it."

"I have a feeling you're right," I said. I slid off the stool and left. I stopped at the front door long enough to check, but the other car wasn't out there. I had a boy bring the Cadillac around and drove off. I checked for three or four blocks but nobody was following me. I drove straight to the dock below Bacci's house. I parked, then stepped aboard the boat and called out. His voice told me to come below.

There he was, as I had seen him the last time. There was a glass of rum in front of him. Also a chess board. He was working out a chess game.

"Whose move is it?" I asked.

"White's. Why?"

"Why don't you move your king's knight's pawn to three and you'll have a checkmate in two more moves?"

He stared at the board for a minute and then glared at me. "Why the hell didn't you tell me you played chess?"

"Why should I? You didn't ask me, and I don't have any time for chess anyway."

He swept the chessmen into a box and looked at me again. "What do you have time for?" he demanded.

"Broads, drinking and business—more or less in that order. Any objections?"

"No," he said with a big sigh. "Just envy, lad. Sit down and have a glass."

"Just one. We have work to do."

"I figured that," he said. He put the box and the board away and poured a glass of rum for me. "Sit down and tell me what we're going to do. I already have the tranquilizers for you."

"I counted on that." I sat down and lifted the glass. "To the miscreant—and his downfall."

"I'll drink to that, lad." We drank and he thumped his glass on the table. "What do we do with him?"

"It's not exactly a chess game," I told him. "And when it's over, nobody is going to tell you that you played well.

149

On the other hand, nobody is going to say you played badly, because you won't be able to hear them. As a result, you play it by ear and hope for the best."

"I understand, lad. I've played such games many a time—in my head. In the university, my specialty was the fourteenth, fifteenth and sixteenth centuries. I gloried in the adventures of that period and participated in them—in my imagination. But I never knew how well I would do in reality."

"We've all done that," I said gently. "And in reality we never know how well we'll do until it's all over. In the meantime, don't be unduly worried. You may be in some danger in the beginning, but that will be only the same kind of danger as on the other run when we were fired at. You do as I tell you to and you will have participated enough."

"Right, lad. What do we do first?"

"First, I go up to my car and get the hamburger. We then make up the special hamburgers for the Dobermans." I went upstairs and got the meat. We made several hamburger balls, each one with tranquilizers inside. Aristotle poured each of us another glass of rum. I lifted my glass. "To our adventure," I said gravely.

He actually beamed as he lifted his glass to drink. "Thank you, lad. Now, what's the plan?"

"The plan is very simple. We go up to the back of his house as before. Only this time we go even quieter and turn off the running lights before we even head in. I want you to get as near the shore as you can and then stay there. We throw the meat over the fence to the dogs and wait until they're out of business. Then I go inside and you wait for me."

"That's all?" he asked in surprise.

"Just about. If I'm real lucky, I might be back, but I don't expect to be that lucky. I'm going to give you a phone number. If you hear any gunshots inside the house, I want you to call that number. It's the home phone of Lieutenant Dillman of the Miami Beach Police. Tell him what is happening and where and tell him I'm inside the house. Tell him I said not to be late."

"That's all?"

"That's enough. Then you get back to your dock as quickly as you can and without being spotted."

"All right," he said unhappily. "But I don't understand it."

"You will afterward." I took my notebook from my pocket and tore out the sheet that had Dillman's number on it. I pushed it across to him. "There's the phone number. Don't lose it whatever you do."

"I won't." He put it away in his shirt pocket and buttoned the flap.

I reached in my pocket, took out fifty dollars and put that on the table. "And put that in your pocket or your sugar can."

"What's that for? You already gave me the second fifty."

"Call it for services over and beyond the call of duty. Or call it a bonus. Just file it under R—for rum."

"All right. What do we do next?"

"We finish our drinks and cast off."

"Just like that, eh? I must remember if we ever get to play that game of chess. Just answer one more question for a bewildered old man, will you, lad? Why didn't you wait to give me the bonus until after this is all over?"

I smiled at him. "That one's easy, Aristotle. I fully expect to finish tonight's little chore standing on my feet, but there's always the chance that someone may throw a banana peel under my heel just at the moment I begin to tango. And I forgot to make a will."

"You mean you think you might get killed?"

"I thought you were a philosopher. I don't plan to be killed, but there are many surprises in front of us. I think everyone is aware that no matter what he does it must one day end in death. Where? When? How? There are answers to everything but that. I have enough ego to think that I will make it through what is about to happen. But I might do so, then go back to the hotel and slip in the bathtub and kill myself. Still no will and no fifty bucks. In other words, I believe in living every day as if it were the first day of the rest of my life—and the last day of my life up to that point. That sums it up."

He shook his head. "I can't quarrel with it as a philosophy, but I'm not sure I could live with it."

"Hell, you are, in a way and have been since you left the university. The only real difference is that I know how to use a gun and you don't."

"Maybe," he said. "But I can see that you want to start moving, so let's get it over with."

"I'm ready," I said.

He went above to cast off and I finished my drink while he was gone. I felt fine, a combination of relaxed and tense. I knew from experience it was the best way to feel. I pulled out both of my guns to check them over while he was gone. Everything was perfect.

Aristotle came back down and started the motor. We moved away from the dock and headed for the big house on low throttle. Before we got there, he cut the running lights. Then as we neared the shore, he cut the motor and we drifted into the landing spot. As we reached it, I heard a slight splash and knew he'd dropped the anchor.

I picked up the balls of hamburger and went above. I could see the Dobermans circling around in the back yard and looking in our direction. I tossed some of the meat over the back fence and watched the dogs start gobbling it up. I waited and watched. It wasn't long before they began to yawn and crouch down for a few seconds before they moved again. I waited and finally they stretched out on the grass and were still. I went below.

"Thanks, Aristotle," I said quietly. "Remember what I told you. I'll see you soon."

"I hope so, lad. Good luck."

I slapped him on the shoulder and went back to the deck. It was an easy jump to the beach. I went up to the big iron gate. I took a small leather case from my pocket. It held a number of very fine lock picks. I selected one and tried it on the padlock. It didn't work. I chose the next size and within seconds the lock opened. I stepped inside the yard, closed the gate gently and walked past the two silent dogs.

There were lights on in one room on the ground floor. There was a patio in front of the room (or maybe it was the back, since it was in the back of the house), and the outer wall was all glass. There were heavy curtains drawn across the glass but as I got closer I saw there was a small opening in the curtains. I went up and discovered that I could see part of the room.

It looked like a playroom or recreation room. I could see the end of a pool table and two slot machines against the wall. There was also a desk, and behind it was Angelo Bacci. He was the same man I had once known in Las Vegas. A little older, a little fatter, but the same. Over to one side, I spotted Carl Ketcher sitting in a large leather chair. That was all I could see of the room.

I moved to the right and found a small door. There was no light beyond it, but I peered through the glass. It looked as if it opened into a hallway. The door was locked, but it was easy to pick. I opened the door and stepped inside, closing it gently behind me. I stood there for a minute, listening. The only sound was one of music coming from somewhere above.

I moved carefully along the hallway until I reached a spot where it branched off. There was a light from somewhere straight ahead, and to the left I could see a thin shaft of light coming from beneath a door. I decided that must be the door to the room I had seen from outside. I started for it.

I had taken no more than six or seven steps when I heard the rustle of movement, and then a hard object was shoved against my back.

"Okay, sucker," the man's voice said. "Just move carefully ahead and open the door. We're both going in, but if you make any sudden move, only one of us is going to make it all the way."

10

Ketcher, I knew, was sitting in a chair in the room, so it must be Hackett behind me. I wasn't really surprised and not at all upset. In fact, I was rather pleased it was turning out this way. I knew they wouldn't kill me at once. Bacci would want to find out how much I knew, and Ketcher and Hackett would enjoy their cat-and-mouse game. I opened the door and stepped inside.

Ketcher was still sitting in the chair, but he was looking at the door. There was a gun in his hand pointing at me, and he had a big smile on his face.

"Come in, sucker," he said.

"Hello, Ketcher," I said. I looked at the man behind the desk. "Hello, Angelo. You do get around, don't you?"

"So do you, March. The last time I saw you was in Las Vegas, but I've never forgotten you. I thought of you every day I spent doing time, and I've thought of you every time I've walked since then."

"Yeah," I said. "Those bullets through the kneecap do refresh the memory, don't they? Why don't we try it on friend Ketcher here? I'll bet he could scream up a pretty song."

"Shut up, March," Ketcher said. "Dan, pull his fangs."

155

Hackett reached around carefully and took my gun from the shoulder holster. Then he patted my sides, my waist and my pockets.

"Don't get too familiar," I said. "You're not exactly my type."

"You're going to be my type before the night's over," he said viciously. "He's clean, Carl."

"Good," said Ketcher. "Why don't you invite him to have a seat, Dan?"

"With pleasure," Hackett said. He racked me across the back of the head with the gun barrel, then shoved me as hard as he could. I staggered across the room and ended up more or less in a leather chair.

"Take it easy," Bacci said. "I want to find out what he knows, and then it's going to take him a long time to die."

"If it's going to take that long," I said, "do you mind if I smoke a cigarette?"

"Go ahead."

I took out a cigarette and lit it. "Nice little joint you got here, Angelo. I guess you've continued to do as well as you were doing when I first met you."

"I'm doing all right," he said.

"You mean you were. Now, it's getting up tight."

Carl Ketcher laughed. "You're a fool March. I'll admit that you're pretty good with a gun when you have the drop, but when you decided to come walking in here, you made your last big mistake. We were wise to you from the time you came around to check up. We knew you'd be back."

"Take a look, Carl," Bacci said.

Ketcher got up and walked over to what looked like a

TV set. He turned it on, and when the screen lighted up, I could see Aristotle's boat bobbing gently just off the back shore. It surprised me, but it also explained why they had fired at us so quickly that first trip.

"Think you're so smart," Ketcher said. "The boss has closed-circuit television and infrared lighting to cover every side of the house."

"Stop talking like a goddamn TV salesman," Bacci snapped. "I told you to take a look, not make a speech."

"It's still there just the way he left it. I told you he must've put the anchor over the side, figuring he could make a getaway in it."

"Okay. What about the dogs?"

"They're still laying on the grass close to the fence."

"What did you do with the dogs, March? Kill them?"

"No," I said. "I fed them tranquilizers. They won't be out too long."

"A good thing. I can't stand people who don't treat dogs right."

"I always said you were a humanitarian, Angelo," I said drily.

"Want us to work him over a little, boss?" Hackett asked.

"When I'm ready, I'll let you know," Bacci said. He turned to look at me. "Who was the broad who left your hotel for the airport just before you cut the boys off on Collins?"

"A friend of mine. Her vacation was over and she had to go back to her job. I thought your trained seals might have seen her with me and would have the bright idea of asking her about me."

"Okay," he said. "Now, what's this all about, March? What do you want?"

"I thought you knew. I've told enough people."

"I mean what's all this nonsense about bonds and about you putting the muscle on everybody because of them?"

"I suppose it was also nonsense about Wilma Leeds being murdered and left in the Everglades?"

"That broad?" he said. "She probably got knocked up and was trying to make the guy marry her, so he handled it that way. How do I know about dizzy broads?"

"You provided an alibi for Jack Daly and Bobby Dixon."

"Who? Oh, you mean those two young guys. Nice kids. I didn't know they needed alibis. They just happened to be over one or two nights playing gin rummy."

"Sure they were. Let's take another killing. Are you going to try to tell me that Speed Harris also got knocked up and was killed by somebody who didn't want to marry him?"

"Speed Harris? Oh, you mean the old jockey? I didn't know he was dead. Used to be a great jockey. Maybe I ought to send some flowers."

"What's wrong, Angelo? Your boys aren't reporting everything to you?"

"What's the meaning of that crack?" Dan Hackett asked.

"I thought it was obvious. I mean you two punks killed him over in Miami. Gunned him down on the street. Like the old days, eh, Angelo? I thought the big boys had decided no more killings like in the old days."

"You're nuts," Ketcher said. "We ain't killed nobody.

158

Why don't we finish him off and get it over with? Some of his cop pals might be following him."

"He doesn't work that way," Bacci said. "I ought to know because I had plenty of time to find out about him while I was waiting for my kneecap to heal up and for my time to be over. And even afterwards. I knew I'd run into him again some time, and I wasn't in any big hurry. But he don't work that close with the cops. I mean he don't let them know what he's doing. He likes to play it alone, and that makes him a big man."

"Maybe he's changed."

Bacci shook his head. "I don't think so. When I got rapped by the Feds, I thought it was because he tipped them off he was meeting me that day. I found out later that they were following him because they didn't trust him, even though he was doing a job for them. We got plenty of time. I want to hear him talk."

"We could help him get the idea. Maybe by shooting him through the kneecap."

"You can't shoot that straight," I said. "Besides I've noticed that most people scream when they're shot there. It might disturb the neighbors in a section like this."

Ketcher made a suggestion about the neighbors. It illustrated his tendency to become rude at times.

"Shut up," Bacci said flatly. "When I want you to shoot him through the kneecap, I'll tell you. Now, March, you're really an insurance investigator, right?"

"Right."

"So he's a lousy insurance cop," said Ketcher.

Bacci didn't even look at him. "I said to shut up! What insurance company do you work for, March?"

"Intercontinental."

"They pay you well?"

"Very well."

"I hate your guts," he said, "for what you did to me."

"You have to admit that I gave you a good deal on that jade."

"I admit it," he said with a tight smile. "But it took me over a year to get it back with a clean bill. But what I was starting to say was that while I hate your guts I admire your style. I wish I could find a few men like you, even one."

"Boss!" Ketcher said.

Bacci just looked at him, and the blond gunman closed his mouth. "Your last chance, Carl," Bacci said. He looked back at me. "How well do they pay you?"

I decided to go along with him and let him have his fun. "Three bills a day, an unlimited expense account and frequent large bonuses. It keeps me in booze, broads and cigarettes."

"How would you like to work for me? I could pay you a lot more than that."

"I don't think I could afford it. Besides I talk back to my present employers and they dummy up."

"I thought that's what you'd say. Okay, you're working on a job down here. Since you talk about it so much, it must have something to do with bonds. Why keep dragging me into it?"

"Because you're into it up to your chin. I'll level with you, Bacci. I'm not sure that you can be convicted of that part of it. But it will cause you some trouble and will make you lose some face with your brothers. I hate to tell a story when I know that the other person already knows it, but if you like I'll tell you about it."

"Go ahead. I'll listen."

"Since you're the host," I said, "how about a drink?"

He waved over toward the closed-circuit TV. "Help yourself."

There was a portable bar there. I walked over and poured myself a generous splash of bourbon and went back to the chair. I lit a cigarette.

"It starts with two broads who worked for a stock brokerage firm in New York. They were young, good-looking broads, but they were lonely. They met two punks named Jack Daly and Bobby Dixon. Daly, especially, is a good-looking guy and a swinger. The broads had access to certain bonds and securities. So they got talked into stealing a few. Worth a million and a half."

"It usually works like that," he said with a smile.

"The broads grab the packet, change their looks and come to Florida. They turn the goods over to Daly and Dixon. Now, I'd guess that Daly is smart enough to figure out that one way of disposing of such things was out because the theft was discovered too soon, which meant that banks would have a record of them. But there is one other way. You sell the goods at a reasonable price to someone who has connections. He in turn sells it to one of his connections, who sells it to another connection and eventually it winds up in Europe."

"You're smart, March," he said. "Maybe too smart. And you're in the wrong racket."

"My blood pressure wouldn't stand the other racket," I said. "But I gather that you're interested in my little story."

"Go ahead."

"Daly and Dixon collect a few dollars. Daly is romancing one of the broads, and Dixon is trying with the other one, but she doesn't dig him. But they give the broads five grand each to keep them quiet. Daly—and I'm only guessing he's the one—is already thinking that the two broads are the only ones who can nail him to the action. He has the answer to that. Get rid of them. The first one is the broad he's shacking with. That one is easy. He takes her on a romantic drive along the Tamiami Trail and kills her. He dumps the body in the swamp and sets up an alibi with a good friend."

"What does he do with the other one?"

"Nothing. He's moved too fast. The other one is a scared little canary, so she changes her looks again and takes a quick hike. Now, the fat's in the fire. He's worried, Dixon is worried and their friend, who gave them the alibi, is worried."

"Sounds reasonable." He motioned, without looking. "Get me a drink, Carl."

The gunman went and brought him a drink. Bacci took it without any recognition of the service. "Go ahead, March."

"Now," I said, "we switch the scene slightly. The goods have been sold to a man in Florida who sells them to another man in, say, Chicago. That man sells them in turn to another man—pick any city, maybe Boston. All of this in a matter of a few short weeks. Clever, one would say. From Boston, it can go to any other city in the country or to Europe. But it didn't."

"Why didn't it?" He held up one hand. "Don't tell me. Let me guess. Because one man somewhere in America either guessed or knew where it was going before it got there?"

"Yes."

"And, I suspect, that one man was you."

"Yes," I said modestly. "Do you happen to know a man called Bicksy Gordon?"

"I've heard of him," he said.

"He was arrested this morning in Boston. You have probably heard the news. In his possession was a bag containing one and a half million dollars worth of missing bonds and securities. With him was a man who had just arrived from Chicago. I doubt if there is any way that Gordon can escape the possession charge. I suspect the man from Chicago can and that the other man in Chicago will go without mention. As will the man in Miami Beach."

He sighed. "I suppose that is the end of the story?"

I took a drink, snubbed out my cigarette and lit another one. "Not quite. As a matter of fact this is where it gets interesting and complicated. You're forgetting a chain of events."

"What?"

"We started out with two broads. Squares who want to be swingers. One of them now dead—the other one not. The two broads are connected with Jack Daly and Bobby Dixon—both quite alive. The one remaining broad can furnish information, which can be checked out, that Daly and Dixon were the receivers, at least, of stolen property. One of the girls is murdered. The obvious suspect is Jack Daly, who was seeing her every night up to the night of the murder. But Jack Daly has an alibi—furnished by a man who *might* have bought the bonds and securities from him. You find this interesting?"

"Very," he said flatly.

163

"Now," I went on, "we approach the complicated part. Daly and Dixon will undoubtedly be charged with planning grand larceny, receiving stolen property, possession of stolen property and the sale of stolen property. In addition, Daly will be charged with murder one, Dixon with being an accessory before and after the fact. And the man with whom they dealt might well be charged with buying, possessing and selling stolen property—and with being an accessory to the murder."

He took a cigar from his desk, lit it and sighed heavily. "That sounds unlikely," he said. "I see no evidence of proof in what you've said."

"But you're forgetting one thing," I said gently. "Our little chain of events. Somewhere in the United States there is still a broad who was involved with the beginning. She can put the finger on Daly and Dixon for the original crime. She can even help to put it on them for the murder.

"Now, Daly and Dixon," I continued, "are not men who go gladly to their doom. Faced with what they have earned, they may try to strike a bargain whereby they talk about the man to whom they sold the bonds and securities and about the man who provided them with an alibi. They may try to put all the blame on each other. And the other man might withdraw the alibi he provided for them, thus making them more desperate and more eager to drag him down with themselves. You see how complicated it becomes?"

"Yeah, I see," he said, "but it seems to me that there's a very simple solution you're overlooking."

"What's that?"

"There's one key that will unlock the whole chain, as

164

you call it. If she doesn't testify against anybody then the chain ends right there. I mean the little broad who is somewhere in the United States—as you said."

"What does that mean?" I asked.

"Nothing special. Just a statement of fact. Let us say that she decides that it is to her advantage not to testify, then the chain of events stops right there."

"Meaning that she takes the rap?"

"That would be one solution," he said.

"You said it might be to her advantage? How?"

"I don't know. I'm just guessing. Somebody might put money in the bank for her every year. Since the bonds and securities are back, she probably wouldn't have to do more than five years. A young broad like that could do it standing on her head and come out with maybe fifty or a hundred grand. She'd be set for life."

"That's what I thought you had in mind," I said. "Let us suppose, for example, that she should decide that she doesn't want to take such a generous offer. What then?"

"Well, I can only guess. It's pretty tough doing time. It can get almost anyone down. And there's always a chance that someone might take a dim view of any kind of a cop-out. Something might happen to her in the jail even before she got sent up for her sentence. Again, there would be no case against anyone. You've been around. You know how things happen."

I finished my drink and put out my cigarette.

"Yeah, I know how things happen. But in this case you would have to find out where she is before much could happen."

"Not me . . . someone. But I imagine that could be arranged."

"How?"

He smiled but there was no humor in it. "You know where she is," he said.

"Sorry, chum, you've got a wrong number. I don't know where the lady is."

"Don't be difficult, March. Forget all the things I said when you first arrived. I was just kidding you then. You tell me where the broad is and we'll forget everything else that's between us."

"Just like that, huh? You'll let me walk right out of here?"

"Yes."

"And your two pet monkeys here?"

"I guarantee you that no one will stop you from walking out of this house."

"I get it," I said. "You mean that no one will stop me from walking—if I *can* walk. Is that it? Sorry, Angelo, old friend, I don't know where she is."

"Hackett," Bacci said without looking around, "see if you can help him to see it my way. But don't be like Ketcher. He loves his work too much. I don't want him to be so he can't talk—just make sure he does talk."

"Sure, boss," Hackett said. He started walking slowly towards me, a smile on his face. He was carrying his gun in his right hand and mine in his left. I got the impression that he loved his work too.

I stood up and waited, watching Hackett closely. Finally he was close to me. He stopped, both feet planted widely apart. He shifted his weight as he swung the gun in his right hand. I tried to duck the full impact of it, but it still hurt as the barrel scraped across the top of my

166

head. I went down on one knee, shaking my head to clear it.

At the same time, I pulled the small gun from the holster taped to my left leg. I looked up. Hackett was no longer smiling, he was grinning. He had lifted the gun and had started to bring it down on top of my head. I steadied the gun and shot him just below his belt.

His body jerked as his grin tightened into a grimace. He dropped the guns automatically, and his hands flashed down to clutch at his groin. Then he fell, first to his knees, then to one side still holding himself. I shifted to face Ketcher.

It was almost too late. He was already swinging his gun into line. If I'd had my own gun I would have snapped a shot at him, because the bullet would have been heavy enough to stop him, but I doubted that the small gun would do that. Instead, I concentrated on the one spot I wanted to hit and squeezed the trigger gently.

We both shot at the same time. I saw the cloth jump at his knee and at the same time felt his bullet slam into my left shoulder. It knocked me back on the floor. I heard another gun go off, then the high-pitched sound from Ketcher's throat.

The third shot must have come from Bacci. I forced myself to sit up and look at him. He was still sitting at the desk, and he was bringing his gun down to sight on me. There was no time to be fancy. Besides, there wasn't too much of him showing. I triggered two bullets as fast as I could into the upper part of his chest. His gun went off and I felt a light blow on the side of my head and then something crashed across the room. Bacci slumped forward on the desk.

167

I looked around the room. Hackett had fainted. Ketcher was lying on the floor, vomiting and groaning. Bacci still had his head on the desk but I could tell he was conscious. His gun was right next to his hand so I collected it first. Then I walked over to Ketcher. He saw me coming and tried to reach his gun on the floor. I gave him a gentle kick in the knee and he fainted. I picked up his gun, then got the two beside Hackett. I just made it to the chair. I was getting a little dizzy myself.

My shoulder was hurting and I could feel the warm blood on it. I looked down. The blood was soaking through my coat, but it didn't look like there was too much of it. Next I explored my head. It was aching and was also bleeding but not enough to worry about.

I got up and managed to reach the portable bar. I poured a stiff drink of bourbon and gulped down half of it. The dizziness began to go away. I filled up the glass and went back to the chair. I took my handkerchief from my pocket, unbuttoned the top of my shirt and put the handkerchief on my shoulder to catch the blood.

Angelo Bacci stirred and used his hands to push himself up from the desk. First he looked for his gun. Then he raised his head and looked around the room, finally staring at me.

"Yeah," I said, "we hit a jackpot. Everybody's wounded, but I'm the only one with guns. Five of them." I thought about that for a minute. "Unless you have another one in that desk. If you do, don't try to get it or I'll make it permanent for you, old chum. Just keep your hands on the desk where I can see them."

"Get the hell out," he said.

"No, thanks. I'm comfortable here."

168

"What do we do now?"

"We wait, baby, just wait," I told him.

He was silent for a minute. "You mean you had cops waiting outside all the time?"

"No, but I did have a friend who was going to call a certain cop if he heard any strange noises from here."

He groaned and looked at me. "This is the second time you've shot me. I won't forget it."

"You weren't going to forget the first time," I said as cheerfully as I could. "You should have a more cheerful outlook, Angelo. Think of it as the fact that I saved your life twice—because I didn't kill you either time. You're ahead of the game."

He called me an unprintable name. "You mean I missed you twice?"

"Not exactly. You did give me a partial haircut but you missed the second one."

"Ketcher?"

"He caught me once and then I'm afraid he immediately came down with the same knee trouble you once had."

"Hackett?"

"He raised a bump on my head before the game ended. I'm afraid he may be in a serious condition. I didn't have time to be selective."

"But they frisked you."

"True. But I'm a big boy and I can carry two guns without listing to port. Now, is there anyone else in the house?"

"Only the broad upstairs," he said, then obviously wished he'd said something else. But he knew it was too late. "She won't come down. She probably didn't even hear anything except that stupid music she plays all the time."

"True love never ran smoother."

"Look, March," he said, "how much would it cost to have you take a hike right now? We can solve our own problems if you're out of the way."

"You couldn't afford it," I told him. "I don't even need that much money. Besides I'll get my jollies out of watching you and your two punks and your two crummy associates getting anything that I can help put on you. Now, shut up. I'm tired of listening to you and I don't feel too good myself."

He kept quiet but I noticed he was watching me, hoping I'd doze off. I felt like it a couple of times but the whiskey helped. It wasn't too long before we heard a siren. It sounded as if it were coming from the water, so they were probably using a boat. The motor stuttered to a stop in the back of the house. I hoped the dogs were still sleeping.

Then two shots rang out. I guessed they hadn't been expected. Bacci was looking toward the glass doors.

"Sorry, Angelo," I said, "but I guess your dogs didn't stay asleep long enough. You should have taught them not to attack cops."

He recited a litany of unprintable phrases. I finished the drink in my glass and got up and walked back to the glass doors. I kept a watch on Angelo. I opened the drapes and stood where I could be seen.

There was a knock on the door and I unlatched it and pulled it back. Lieutenant Dillman came in, followed by several men.

"You look great, Milo," he said. "What's up?"

"I'll tell you later. We have three little friends in here who need medical attention. I don't think they need much restraint, but if you have to, you can temporarily charge them with trying to kill me."

Dillman nodded to his men and they moved in quickly. They put handcuffs on Bacci and carried the other two out. I gave the three guns to Dillman.

"You come along with us," he said. "I think you need a little medical attention yourself. We already have an ambulance waiting. From the remarks of the man who called, I thought we'd need it."

"Where's your ambulance?" I asked.

"Down by the dock. Only a few yards from here. You're sure you're all right?"

"Positive. I asked because my car is parked down there. I have a stop to make before I go to the hospital."

"You're not making any stops."

"Am I under arrest, Lieutenant?"

"No, damn it, but you've got to get to the hospital. From the looks of you, you're losing a lot of blood."

"Always had too much blood anyway. I'm going. It won't take long."

"Idiot!" he said. "If you insist on going, then I'm going with you."

"Wayne," I said patiently, "you know you can't go in with me. I'm only trying to help your case, but I might just bend the law a little bit and you can't be a witness to it. If you want to follow and stay outside until I either show up or you hear a disturbance, okay. But that's all."

I think he swore under his breath but I couldn't make it out, so I ignored it. The police boat swung into the dock only a few yards away from the *Aristotle*. It was in berth, but there was no sign of life except for lights below deck. Bacci and his men were quickly unloaded and put into a waiting ambulance. The attendant looked at me.

"What about him?" he asked. "He looks like he was ripe."

"He," Dillman said strongly, "is a stubborn jackass and he's not going. Johnson, Sorenson, you both come with me. The rest of the men go with the ambulance and see the men are booked."

I walked with all the dignity I could muster to the Cadillac. I got in and pulled away from the dock. I saw that the unmarked police car was following me.

It took only a few minutes over the causeway to the apartment where Jack Daly and Bobby Dixon lived. I parked the car and went upstairs without looking back. I knocked on their door and waited.

I heard movement inside, and then the door opened three or four inches and Jack Daly looked out. I kicked the door as hard as I could and he went back out of sight. I walked in and closed the door behind me. He was standing just a few feet away, holding his hand to his face—but I didn't see any blood.

"What the hell do you want, March?" he asked.

"You, baby. I told you I was coming to see you. Where's your partner?"

"How the hell do I know?"

"Sit down," I told him, pointing to a chair. "I want to talk to you about the death of a girl named Wilma Leeds."

He sat down. "I've been through all that with the cops. I wasn't with her that night. I can prove it."

"Not anymore, baby," I said. "I just shot Angelo

Bacci." I saw his eyes flicker to a spot over my right shoulder. I pulled my gun from the shoulder holster.

"Tell your partner," I said without looking around, "that there's no way he can kill me without you being killed at the same time. And tell him quick. I'm impatient."

"Okay, Bobby," Daly said. "Forget it and come on in."

Dixon moved into view, a gun hanging limply from his hand. He was a skinny guy with shifty eyes and lank blond hair.

"Drop the gun," I said. He dropped it. I noticed he was staring at my shoulder.

"You're wounded," he said.

"Yeah, I'm wounded. And I shot Angelo Bacci and his two hoods, Ketcher and Hackett. They're not walking around and I am. So, Daly, your alibi is gone. You want to know something else?"

"What?" Daly asked. His voice was hoarse.

"Jane Carlton is not only alive, but in a safe place where you couldn't get to her even if you had an army. She can tie you to the bonds and to Wilma Leeds. Bacci isn't going to help you. He has to save himself and that's partly by claiming he had nothing to do with you or the bonds.

"You and Dixon here are going to be arrested for planning a grand larceny, for receiving stolen property, possession of stolen property and the sale of stolen property. In addition, you, Daly, will be charged with murder one in the death of Wilma Leeds, and Dixon will be charged with an accessory before and after the fact to the murder of Wilma Leeds."

"Wait a minute," cried Dixon, "they can't charge me with anything like that!"

"Can't they? You must have known about it before and you were certainly part of the alibi—which is now going to be repudiated by Bacci. You're in it, too, baby, up to your ears."

"To hell with you," Daly shouted. With that, he dived for the gun Dixon had dropped.

I shot in the general direction of the gun. Daly yelped as he hit the floor and I saw there was a red streak on his wrist. But he rolled over and curled up like a pussy cat.

"I'll see both of you in court," I said. I turned and walked out. On the way down the stairs, I met Lieutenant Dillman running up.

"They're both up there," I said. "Daly has a superficial wound on his wrist and they have a gun. They're ripe, Wayne. Charge them with anything and everything you can think of and keep them separated. Work hard on Dixon. He's scared about being involved in the murder rap. I'll fill you in at the hospital."

"Okay," he said quickly. "Johnson is going to drive you there in your car. And keep your mouth shut until the doctors get through with you."

I nodded and walked down the stairs. One of Dillman's men was waiting at my car. I turned over the keys to him and let him drive me to the hospital. I knew I almost passed out as we drove there, but I managed to walk in under my own steam.

They got my clothes off in a few seconds and some doctor began fooling around with my shoulder. I didn't feel much, but then the next thing I knew I was stretched out

174

on an operating table, and some guy was standing over me with something he was about to press down on my face. I started to protest, but a curtain of darkness fell over me before I could say anything.

11

When I came out of it, I was in a bed staring up at a white ceiling. It took me a couple of minutes to remember I was in a hospital. Next I was aware that there was a bottle suspended in the air on either side of me. Tubes hung down from them, and the needles at the end of the tubing were stuck in my arms.

"Well, we're awake, are we?" a cheerful voice asked.

I turned my head and saw a nurse standing next to the bed. She was young and had a pretty face. That was about all I could tell. Those uniforms don't do a thing for a girl's figure.

"Are we?" I asked. "I wasn't quite sure. I thought those bottles might be full of embalming fluid."

She laughed politely. "I can see that you're feeling better. Lieutenant Dillman is waiting to see you."

"Tell him to tiptoe in."

She left the room and he came right in. "Sorry I forgot to bring flowers," he said. "They weren't sure whether you'd survive, so I didn't want to waste the money."

"To hell with you," I said. "Tell them to empty those

two bottles and refill them with my favorite brands. What the hell did they put me on that operating table for?"

"To operate."

"But I didn't need my appendix taken out."

"The bullet was still in your shoulder," he said, "so they took it out. You lost a lot of blood before you got here and that's why you're getting the transfusion. I told them to add a little Geritol to it."

"I get all the funny lines here," I said sharply. "Where's our five customers?"

"Daly and Dixon are in prison cells. Separate ones. The other three are in the hospital under guard. Bacci will come through all right. Ketcher will be all right, but he won't run any races. Hackett is in bad shape. The doctor isn't sure he'll live. We're going to try to get a death-bed confession out of him."

"Work on Dixon, too. It never occurred to him that he might be tied into the murder. I also pointed out to them that Bacci would probably change his story that provided them with an alibi. So Dixon is a good bet to cop out on Bacci and possibly on Daly. I think Daly might even cop out on Bacci if he thinks he can make a deal on the murder. It's worth a try."

"Yeah. Where's the girl, Milo?"

"In New York City under protective custody. She gave herself up today in New York."

"She was the one who took the plane at noon?"

"Yeah."

He swore. "Some cooperation. Where was she?"

I smiled at him. "In my hotel. Don't worry. She's not

177

being kept from you but from them. You want to know the whole story?"

"Not now. We'll get it in the morning. I don't think we will question them tonight. Let them sweat a little. In the meantime, they are all charged with assault with a deadly weapon and attempted murder on you. That'll hold them until tomorrow. I'll see you early in the morning."

"Just one more thing," I said. "Is this a private room or is it on the city?"

"Private. They must have counted your money when they took your pants off. Good night, Milo."

"If it's a private room and I'm paying for it, send the nurse in as you go out."

"Watch it, boy. You're in no shape to wrestle." He was gone before I could think of an answer.

The nurse came in almost immediately. "Can I do anything to make you comfortable?" she asked.

"You can. To start with, get these damn needles out of me."

She came over and looked at the bottles. "You've had enough," she said. She removed the needles, put alcohol on the punctures and wheeled the bottles away.

"You seem to have recovered pretty well," she said. "Only be careful with that left arm. It's bandaged pretty tightly but don't make any special effort to move it. Anything else?"

"Yeah. Several things. This is a private room in a private hospital and I'm paying the bill, right?"

"Yes."

"Does the hospital have a name?"

"Yes. It's the Foster Memorial Hospital. The detective who brought you in said you could afford it."

"I didn't ask you if I could afford it. I want a telephone put in here as quickly as possible."

"All right. That can be done in about five minutes."

"Order it done and come back. I want to know other things."

She scurried out and was soon back. She was still trying to look stern and professional but she was obviously enjoying it. "Yes, Mr. March?"

"Since it's a private room and I'm paying for it, I presume I can have visitors any hour I wish?"

"Yes, but you should take it easy. You shouldn't get excited."

"I'm not excited now, but I will be if I don't get what I want. I had two guns on me when I was brought in here. Where are they?"

"The officer said it was all right to let you keep them, so they are in your closet. Your clothes are there, too."

"I also had a number of personal things in various pockets, including some money. Are they in the closet, too?"

"No. All personal things are in a large envelope in the drawer of that table right next to you."

"How's the food in here?"

"Very good. We also have a special menu for private patients. It has almost everything on it that you could get in a regular restaurant. You can get service for another two hours."

I was getting in a better humor. "One more question. May I have a guest to dinner?"

"Well . . . it's not customary, but there's no regulation against it."

"Okay. Now, just see that I get my telephone. Don't forget to smile, baby. I can't stand grouchy nurses."

She laughed. "That's good. I can't stand grouchy patients." She started out, and just then a man arrived with the telephone. He plugged it in and they both left.

I viewed my little domain with some pleasure. There was a little pain in my shoulder, but not enough to bother me unduly. I picked up the phone and gave the operator the number I wanted. The call was soon answered by a girl, but it sounded like the wrong one, so I asked for Annette Rawson. She came on a moment later.

"Milo," I said.

"I was beginning to worry about you. I called the hotel but they didn't know when to expect you. Are you there now?"

"Not quite, honey. There's been a slight change in our plans for the night."

"What?"

"I'm in a hospital. Nothing serious and nothing contagious. I'm in a private room in a private hospital and I'm told they have an excellent private kitchen. Would you mind coming over and having dinner with me here?"

"What happened?"

"I cut myself while shaving. Do you want to come?"

"Of course I do. Where are you?"

"The Foster Memorial Hospital. I don't know exactly where it is, but I imagine a cab driver will know. Oh, yes, there is one more thing. Do you have a fairly large handbag?"

"Yes. Why?"

"They may have an excellent kitchen, but I don't think they have a bar. Bring along a bottle of gin, one of vermouth and we can have martinis. We may have to drink them out of water glasses, but they'll still be martinis."

"Okay, darling. I'll be right there." She hung up. People were hanging up on me again. But in this case I didn't mind.

Next, I put in a call to Aristotle Murphy through the marine operator. He answered on the first ring.

"Milo," he exclaimed. "Are you all right, lad?"

"Almost. I would have phoned you earlier but it was impossible."

"Where are you, lad?"

"The Foster Memorial Hospital. I was just operated on but everything is fine. Nothing to worry about. Why don't you come and see me sometime tomorrow?"

"I will that, lad," he said. "It makes me feel a lot better to know that you're all right. Anything I can bring you?"

"Bring your chess set. I'm not going to be here any longer than I can help. If you think you can sneak it in, you might bring some grog."

"That I will. See you tomorrow." He hung up.

I made two more phone calls. Long distance ones. The first was to Martin Raymond at his home. I told him roughly what had happened and that the bonds and securities had been recovered. It made him so happy he had no criticism of me being in the hospital, although he knew it meant more items on the expense account.

Then I phoned Johnny Rockland at home. "Johnny,"

I said when he answered, "this is Milo. The girl got there all right?"

"Yeah. You know I would've phoned if she hadn't. What's the idea of calling me at home?"

"Just thought I'd let you know what's happened." I gave him a fast run-down on everything up to the moment.

"Good," he said. "I'll call Dillman the first thing in the morning. Where are you now?"

"In the hospital, but I'll be back in a day or two."

"What are you doing in a hospital?"

"Resting my nerves. Good night, Johnny." I hung up.

Annette arrived shortly afterward. She kissed me and started to make a fuss about me being in the hospital.

"Dummy up," I told her. "The important thing is where is the booze?"

She laughed and opened her handbag. She produced a bottle of gin and a bottle of vermouth—and then two martini glasses. I was so pleased that I demanded she kiss me again. She did with such enthusiasm that I almost forgot about my shoulder.

"You'd better watch it," I said. "This isn't a balcony, and we might shock the nurse if she came in suddenly."

"You're just a big fraud," she said. "As badly as you're wounded, you couldn't do anything about it anyway."

"Don't be too sure," I told her darkly. "I've been stretched out here thinking about methods. How do you know how badly I'm wounded?"

"I've already had a conversation with your nurse and she told me. She's bringing us some ice cubes, by the way."

"By the way of where? London?"

Before I could get an answer, the door opened and the nurse came in. Not only did she have the ice cubes but she had managed to get a large glass we could mix them in. And menus.

"I gather you two know each other," I said drily.

"Oh, yes," the nurse said brightly. "We had a lovely conversation. You're a very lucky man, Mr. March."

"That's why I'm here," I said. "Would you like a drink, nurse?"

"It's against the rules," she said. Then she smiled. "Maybe later, if you're still serving."

"We'll be serving," I said.

We looked at the menus and both ordered filet mignon steak. The nurse went off with the order and Annette mixed two martinis. Mine tasted good. The second one was better.

Our dinner came and was as good as the nurse had said it would be. Annette had to cut up my steak for me, but she didn't mind and I certainly didn't.

The nurse did come in for a drink later and so did several other nurses. Finally, the gin ran out and they left us alone.

"I'd better go, darling," she said a few minutes later. "I'm flying back to New York tomorrow. I have a few things to do and I want to come and see you in the morning."

"Okay," I said. "What flight are you on?"

"Twelve o'clock."

"Have breakfast with me in the morning."

"I will," she promised. She kissed me and left. When she was gone I called the airline and made a reservation on the twelve o'clock flight.

I had already decided. The case was over. Everyone would scream, but I wasn't going to stay in the hospital. After Annette had breakfast with me in the morning, I'd talk her into going to the hotel and packing my things. Then I'd be back in New York and could relax—with her. If she got stuffy about it, I could always call Carmen O'Brien, the new receptionist at Intercontinental. After all, I was an invalid and needed to be pampered.